HASHKNIFE AND
THE FANTOM RIDERS

HASHKNIFE AND THE FANTOM RIDERS

W.C. TUTTLE

WILDSIDE PRESS

INTRODUCTION

I first discovered the westerns of Wilbur C. Tuttle (1883–1969)—who wrote prolifically for the pulp magazines of the early 20th century as W.C. Tuttle—in the pages of *Adventure* magazine, where he seemed to have a never-ending stream of excellent stories, all set in the old west. In fact, I later discovered he had published almost a thousand novels and stories, nearly all of which were westerns. This makes him one of the most prolific western writers of all time. He was also a screenwriter beginning in the silent era. He wrote the screenplays for 52 films between 1915 and 1945.

Many of his stories—such as this one—featured Hashknife Hartley, a wandering cowpoke who always seemed to find trouble wherever he went. His best friend and constant companion was "Sleepy" Stevens, who just wanted to settle down and have a ranch of their own. One season of a Hashknife Hartley radio series was produced in 1950-51, but it failed to gain much attention.

Other characters Tuttle created included Cultus Collins, Sad Sontag, and Henry Harrison Conroy, a former vaudeville actor turned sheriff.

Although he published in many different places, including *Short Stories*, *Exciting Western*, and *Boy's Life* (to name just a few), Tuttle's primary market was *Adventure*. In a 1930 poll of, its readers, Tuttle was voted its most popular writer. Fellow western author and editor Jeff Sadler stated Tuttle's writing is "at its best" in the Hashknife stories. Sadler also claims Tuttle's novel *Vanishing Brands* is his finest novel: "...terse and dramatic, flecked with dry touches of wit, the novel is an excellent example of the Western form and a credit to its author."

He was born in Montana, a setting he drew on for many of his stories, and died in Los Angeles County, California.

—John Betancourt
Cabin John, Maryland

CHAPTER I

A COLD drizzle of fog and rain was sweeping in from the ocean, almost obliterating the guttering arc-lights along the street. Far away sounded the clanking rattle of a cable-car, screeching around the sharp turns. An iron-tired vehicle rattled over the cobble-stones, and from far down the harbor sounded the harsh notes of a foghorn.

At the front door of an old-fashioned residence, which had been a magnificent edifice in its time, stood two men, hump-shouldered in the dripping rain. It was impossible, in that light, to describe their appearance, except that one was tall and the other very profane.

The tall one, ignoring the call-button, hammered on the door with his knuckles. They listened for a few moments, and then the smaller one cleared his throat harshly.

"Aw, to hell with this country!"

"Raise yuh a stack of blues," said the tall one dryly.

"'F I ever get out of here—say, 'Hashknife,' are yuh sure this is the place?"

The tall one hammered on the door again, before he said—

"I betcha it is, Sleepy; but the house is so danged big they can't hear m' knock."

As he started to knock again the door opened softly and a butler, of very dignified appearance, squinted closely at them.

"Is this him?" queried the smaller of the two men, but the tall one ignored the question and spoke directly to the butler.

"I been hammerin' on the door for ten minutes."

"Pardon me, but you should have rung, sir."

"Yeah?" The tall man grinned widely. "Well, I might 'a' whistled, but I'll be danged if I ever carried a bell. Is Mr. William Lanpher to home?"

"Yes, sir. Are you Mr. Hartley?"

"M' name's Hartley, yessir."

"Mr. Lanpher is expecting you, sir. He will see you in the library."

"My gosh!" exploded the smaller man, "I hope he don't ask me to read. You go ahead, Hashknife, and I'll guard the rear."

Together they followed the butler into the richly furnished home, where their soggy, high-heeled boots made no sound in the heavy carpets, and into a high-ceiled, homey-looking room, where a log fire crackled in the big fireplace.

"May I take your hats?" asked the butler.

"No, never mind," grinned Hashknife Hartley. "If we stay long, I reckon we can hang 'em up ourselves. Did yuh say he was lookin' for us?"

"Mr. Lanpher will be down in a moment," assured the butler, as he silently withdrew.

The tall man rubbed his big hands together and went to the fireplace, the water still dripping from his wide sombrero. The other man looked around the room, taking in all the details before joining the tall man at the fire, where they stood with their backs to the grateful heat and took stock of the place.

"What do yuh reckon he wants, Hashknife?" asked the smaller man softly.

"I dunno, 'Sleepy.' You seen the letter he sent to us at Phoenix. The secretary of the Cattle Association said that he knowed Lanpher and that he was all right. Danged if I'd 'a' ever come to Frisco if I knowed it was so cold here. Rather face a Dakota blizzard than that danged fog."

"Lanpher must have money," observed Sleepy Stevens. "'F I had money I'd live in the sunshine, y'betcha. I'm wet plumb through. Listen to this—"

Sleepy extended a soggy boot and worked his toes.

"Hear her squirsh?"

Hashknife grinned softly, which almost concealed his eyes in a mass of wrinkles. His face was thin and bony—almost sad in repose, and bronzed to the texture of leather from facing the weather of the wide places.

His arms were long and ended in a pair of muscular hands, which seemed to be always in his way. Sleepy Stevens was shorter, heavier built, with a, deeply-lined face, a calculating pair of blue eyes, and hair which might be designated as a roan color.

Their garb and actions showed plainly that they were from the cattle country, although they were wearing "store" clothes, except for their boots and hats.

"Yeah, I'll admit that yore feet are wet," smiled Hashknife, "but you ain't got nothin' on me, cowboy. I'll bet yuh even money that I've got more water in my boots than you have, and settle it right here."

"Feller, you've done made a bet!" snorted Sleepy, and sat down on the floor, tugging at his boot.

Hashknife leaned against the mantel, hooked the heel of one boot over the toe of the other and began to remove his boot, when William Lanpher came into the room.

So engrossed were the two cowboys that they did not see him until he said—

"Perhaps I can find some dry foot-gear for you."

"Huh!" Hashknife stopped and stared at him. "Howdy. Say, you can referee this bet."

"Bet?" Lanpher stared at them. "I do not understand."

William Lanpher was a medium-sized man, of about fifty years of age, rather fleshy, round-faced and well-dressed. The cities are full of William Lanphers.

"Well," Hashknife grinned softly and looked at his partner, "I reckon we was a little hasty. I bet Sleepy that my feet were wetter than his, but I plumb forgot to state the size of m' bet."

"Write yore bet, cowboy!" snorted Sleepy. "I've got half of it up to m' hip right now, but I'll almost give yuh odds on what's left in m' boot."

Hashknife worked his foot back into his boot, and Sleepy, seeing that the bet was all off, swore softly and scuffed his foot on an expensive Oriental tug, trying to force the boot back on to his foot.

"You are Mr. Hartley," said William Lanpher, "and I have been expecting you."

"I betcha," nodded Hashknife. "But yore front door is so thick that m' knock never got through it."

"I wrote to the Cattlemen's Association," said Lanpher slowly. "I wanted the best man they could recommend."

"You got both of 'em, mister," Sleepy grinned and felt of his toes.

"I only asked for one," smiled Lanpher.

"The good ones comes in sets of twos," said Sleepy seriously.

"The letter was sent to us at Phoenix," said Hashknife. "I know Bill Wheaton, the secretary, real well, and he said he knowed you. We had a hell of a time findin' this house. Me and Sleepy got on one of them danged street-cars that goes clipity-blippin' along, and we hit a curve and Sleepy fell off and—"

"Fell off!" snorted Sleepy. "I got bucked off, yuh mean. The conductor yelped, 'Look out fer the curve!' But he yelped after I was reachin' for the saddle-horn."

"And I got off to pick up the remains, and the danged car went away without us. Sleepy said he'd be darned if he'd ride another one; so we walked."

"We waded," corrected Sleepy.

Lanpher laughed and drew some chairs up to the fire, after which he offered them cigars, but they declined in favor of their own home-rolled cigarets. Lanpher, once he got settled in his chair, lost no time in coming down to his reasons for sending for them.

"I own a half-interest in the Circle Cross cattle outfit in the Ghost Hills Range. Know where it is?"

"I know where it's located," nodded Hashknife, "but we ain't never been there. I've heard of the Circle Cross outfit."

"I wish I never had," said Lanpher bitterly. "It has already cost me a fortune in money, and," he hesitated, "has cost me more than mere money could replace."

"Cow ranches are expensive sometimes," agreed Sleepy interestedly.

"What seemed to be the real trouble with the Circle Cross?" queried Hashknife, stretching his long legs out to the fire and rolling another cigaret.

Lanpher tossed his cigar into the flames and leaned back in his chair.

"Three years ago," he began, "Jim Trainor and I bought the Circle Cross. Trainor knew the cattle business—I had the money. It was sort of a case of him putting his experience against my cash. We bought stock from all over Wyoming, and I will assure you that the outlay of gold was considerable. I knew nothing about the business, but I knew that Jim did. In fact, I know nothing about it now, except that—well, my experience was not exactly pleasant.

"One year ago, or about that length of time, the Circle Cross cattle began to disappear. Perhaps it was longer ago than that, but no matter. A roundup proved that we had lost a small fortune in cattle.

"Jim started an investigation, but was unable to arrive at any conclusion. But it served to increase his vigilance and he found that stock was disappearing with startling regularity."

"Some smart rustlers cleanin' yuh out, eh?" smiled Sleepy. "They will do things like that, Mr. Lanpher."

"So we discovered," said Lanpher dryly. "After our own investigations failed, we called upon the Cattlemen's Association, and they sent an operative. He worked as a cowboy upon the Circle Cross, but was unable to solve the mystery.

"He was taken off the job and another man put on. This man was shot and killed a week after he went into the Ghost Hills country. He was found, riddled with bullets, lying in a corral just outside the town of Wolf Wells. There was no clue to his death. Another detective was sent in to take his place."

Lanpher paused to light a cigar and Hashknife snuggled deeper into his big chair.

"Does it interest you?" asked Lanpher.

"We ain't made no move to walk out," grinned Hashknife. "Keep her spinnin', pardner."

Lanpher nodded slowly and squinted into the fire.

"I'm no story teller, Hartley. This might be embellished quite a lot, but I haven't the ability to use words. That detective was there ten days when he was killed—shot."

"One detective was taken off the job and the next two were killed, eh?" mused Hashknife thoughtfully. "Two out of three is a pretty good average. Was you there, Lanpher?"

"No. This last killing was done a month ago. It seemed a foolish thing to ask the association to send in another man; so I corresponded with Mr. Wheaton. He advised me to get in touch with you."

"Did the sheriff arrest anybody?" queried Sleepy. "They mostly always does arrest somebody."

Lanpher threw his cigar into the fire and leaned forward, elbows on knees, squinting thoughtfully, as if trying to frame a reply. Then he nodded slowly, seriously.

"Yes, they arrested old 'Pinto' Cassidy."

Lanpher shut his jaws tightly and got to his feet. He seemed to be laboring under a strain, as he paced half the length of the room before turning back to them. Hashknife and Sleepy waited for him to resume.

"And that is the part of the whole thing that hurts," he said slowly. "Cassidy is a squawman. His wife is a Sioux squaw. He owns the Tomahawk outfit. God knows, he had enough Indian about his place, without using a tomahawk for a brand."

"You know him very well?" asked Hashknife.

Lanpher ignored the question.

"Cassidy had forbidden any of the Circle Cross outfit to come on to the Tomahawk ranch. This detective was working on the Circle Cross, and he was found dead within quarter of a mile of the Tomahawk ranch-house. He was on Cassidy's ranch.

"But it is doubtful whether they can convict him, and if they do, it will not bring our cattle back. I do not think that Cassidy is the rustler. It is not a one-man job, Hartley, and requires more brains than any squawman has. In fact, we haven't the slightest idea where the stock has gone. That will be your job—to find out."

"And duck bullets," added Hashknife grinning. "You ask quite a lot, mister man. But you ain't told us everythin'. What is yore big interest in Cassidy?"

"Interest!" Lanpher fairly spat the word, as he reached into a pocket and drew out an envelope.

For a moment he hesitated, but drew out the letter and handed it to Hashknife.

"I think that will explain it to you," he said evenly.

The letter was post-dated at Wolf Wells, and read:

> Dad, you might as well save your breath and make the best of things. Regardless of what you say or do, I am going to stick with Cassidy. And what is more, I am going to marry Lorna one of these days. I haven't seen any of the boys of the Circle Cross for quite a while.
>
> I suppose I am to be classed with Cassidy's alleged bunch of rustlers, as you intimated in your letter. Well, all right, I don't mind. This is a wide, wide world and I am twenty-one.
>
> Your affectionate son,
>
> Ben.

Hashknife folded up the letter and handed it back to Lanpher.

"Do you understand what it means?" queried Lanpher hoarsely.

"Who's Lorna?"

"Cassidy's daughter—a half-breed."

"Well," Hashknife frowned for a moment and looked up at Lanpher with a quizzical smile.

"She ain't never scalped anybody, has she?"

"Scalped?" Lanpher stared at Hashknife. "Why—uh—does this appear as something—er—funny?"

Lanpher's face was red with indignation.

"Not exactly funny," agreed Hashknife, serious again. "But I don't see where you ought to chaw up yore own shirt over it, Lanpher."

"You don't? Do you think I want my son to marry an Indian?"

"She's only half-Indian."

"All right, half-Indian! I don't want her!"

"Well! You ain't gettin' her, are yuh?" blurted Sleepy. "He said it was a wide, wide world and—"

"Wide world, fiddlesticks! He talks big, because he thinks he's a man. Bennie wants to pose. A martyred son, and all that kind of rubbish. Marry that damn Indian? I guess not."

"Pardner, yo're doin' a lot of guessin'," smiled Hashknife. "This here love thing is a funny old bug. Ain't nobody ever found a cure for it. And as far as the Injun girl is concerned, she's half-American."

"Her father is Irish as Paddy's pig!"

"Her mother is American," reminded Hashknife softly.

Lanpher scowled into the fire and nodded slowly.

"That's true."

Hashknife yawned and got to his feet.

"Well Sleepy, I reckon we better be goin'."

"Yeah," agreed Sleepy sourly, "we'll be wadin' back down the hill."

"But we haven't come to any agreement," protested Lanpher. "You'll take the job, won't you?"

Hashknife shook his head.

"I don't think so. It ain't noways a healthy place to horn into, and if three cattle detectives have failed, I don't see where two ordinary punchers stand a chance."

"Afraid?" Lanpher's voice was slightly contemptuous.

"Very likely," agreed Hashknife dryly.

"And Wheaton said you had the nerve of the devil. I'll show you his letter."

"But he neglected to say that we also placed quite a value on our own heads," grinned Hashknife. "Still, it might not be as bad as it looks, Sleepy. Yo're always honin' for action, cowboy; suppose we take this job."

"Then don't blame me if we both get killed, Hashknife."

"That's fine!" applauded Lanpher. "I'll pay you one thousand dollars apiece to tackle the job. If you show me where our cattle have gone, I'll double it. I don't know you, but Wheaton said you were the only one—"

"I'm goin' to whip Bill Wheaton for lyin' about me," interrupted Hashknife. "There's two liars in Arizona, and Bill Wheaton is both of them."

Lanpher laughed as he crossed to a table and wrote two checks.

"That will be the best money I ever spent, I think," he remarked, as he banded them to the two cowboys.

"We'll use the word 'most,'" grinned Sleepy, squinting at the check. It was the biggest check he had ever seen.

"Pay to the order of Sleepy Stevens, one thousand dollars. Holy henhawks! I betcha I won't sleep a wink."

"Now, don't go and spend it foolishly," laughed Lanpher.

"Nossir." Sleepy folded it and shoved it deep in his pocket. "That stays right in the old poke until I can find a place where they sell rubber-boots."

They were laughing when the butler came in, apologetic for the intrusion, and spoke a man's name to Lanpher.

"Tell him I'll be out in a moment, Parker."

"Well, we'll be movin'," said Hashknife, picking up his hat. "T'morrow we'll head for the Ghost Hills, Lanpher."

"Fine. I'll wire Trainor tonight and tell him to—"

"Nope." Hashknife stopped him. "You lay off that stuff. Me and you and Sleepy are the only ones that need to know. There's a danged smooth gang in there, Lanpher. Remember, they spotted them detectives."

"Well, that's true, Hartley."

Lanpher shrugged his shoulders.

"Go ahead and do it in your own way."

He led the way out of the room, and as they neared the front door, a man stepped over and spoke to Lanpher. He was a well-dressed, thin-featured man, slightly gray at the temples and with a trifle of a limp in his right leg.

"Good evening, Mr. Lanpher," he said, and nodded to the two cowboys.

"Hello, Carsten," Lanpher held out his hand cordially, and then introduced Hashknife and Sleepy.

"Mr. Carsten is a cattle-buyer," he explained.

Hashknife nodded and held out his hand to Lanpher, just as the front door opened and in came two richly dressed women. One of them was a slender, imperious-looking young lady, and the other a middle-aged woman, rather fleshily built.

Carsten spoke cordially to both of them, and Lanpher smilingly said—

"Mrs. and Miss Lanpher, I want you to meet Mr. Hartley and Mr. Stevens.

"And we're sure pleased t' meetcha," grinned Hashknife, shaking hands with both of them, although it was obvious that neither of the ladies cared for the handshaking.

"We're just makin' a short call," explained Hashknife. "Thought we'd kinda wade out to see Lanpher before leavin' town."

No one seemed inclined to pick up the conversation; so Hashknife said—

"We're sure pleased t' meetcha, and if yuh ever drift over into our country, drop in and see us."

The ladies murmured something conventional, but Carsten elevated his eyebrows a trifle, as he said—

"Just where is your country, Hartley?"

"Well," grinned Hashknife, "yuh might say it was anywhere in the Western side of the U. S. A."

"Sort of drifters, eh?"

"Nope."

Hashknife shook his head.

"We travel under our own power, Carsten. Good night, folks."

They went out of the front door and into the fog and rain. The fog-horns were sending out their eerie wailings down on the harbor, and the street lights gleamed dully at close quarters or faded to mere halo-like spots at a few yards distant.

The two cowboys halted on the sidewalk and tamed their backs to the drifting elements.

"What do yuh make of it, Hashknife?" asked Sleepy, his teeth chattering in spite of himself.

"I dunno what to make of it, Sleepy; but we've already made two thousand dollars out of it. Here comes one of them rattlety-bump cars, goin' downtown. Do yuh think yuh can ride her on the curves?"

"I'll ride inside and lock m' heels," declared Sleepy. "My gosh, ain't Miss Lanpher a dinger. Whooee! The queen of Sheber never had anythin' on her—except a snake."

CHAPTER II

IT WAS very hot in the town of Wolf Wells, a huddle of unpainted buildings, strung more or less along a crooked, dusty street. Wolf Wells was strictly a cattle town, where no one seemed inflicted with too much morals, and its temperature was very hot in Summer and below zero in Winter, which probably accounted for the weather-beaten appearance of the whole place.

A branch railroad wound its crooked way through the Ghost Hills to Wolf Wells, but the train service seemed in the hands of the train crews, rather than in any semblance of a schedule. Wolf Wells was the county-seat.

Just now the town was fairly well-filled with people. It was Saturday, which accounted for some of the activity, but the majority of the people were interested in the outcome of Pinto Cassidy's trial for murder.

The jury, a bunch of hard-bitten cattlemen, were still deliberating, after thirty hours of being locked up in a hot jury-room. Near one of the hitch-racks stood Jim Trainor, half-owner of the Circle Cross outfit, talking to "Fat" Fleager, the sheriff.

Trainor was a big man, broad of shoulder and with a face that was as inflexible as a piece of granite. His eyes were gray, like the gray of tempered steel, and his jaw jutted belligerently, as he bit reflectively at his lower lip.

The sheriff was built after the manner of a bed-slat, and from the sadness of his thin face, the bloodhound-like eyes, with their heavy pouches, one might well expect him to be the proprietor of a non-paying undertaking establishment.

Both men were dressed in range clothes, and Fat Fleager seemed to be continually in danger of losing his belt, which hung draped around his narrow hips. The waistband of his overalls Seemed to cause him much concern also, and the arm-holes of his vest continually crawled out over the paints of his narrow shoulders.

They were both looking at a young man, dressed in cowboy garb, who crossed the street past them and went into a saloon. He was a slender young man, unshaven, unhandsome, but there was a devil-may-care slouch to his walk and to the angle of his sombrero. He did not look at Trainor and the sheriff.

"There's a damn fool that's breedin' a scab for himself," said Trainor, as the young man passed into the saloon.

"Yeah." The sheriff nodded wearily. "I s'pose."

"No brains. Old man's got lots of money. Damn kid could pick out a society girl for a wife, but he ain't got no brains."

"Lanpher got lots of money?" Indifferently.

"Ought to have."

"Rich kid come to cowland and learned papa's business, eh?" The sheriff actually smiled at his own humor.

"Lanpher ought to come out here and kick the kid back to Frisco," growled Trainor.

"Uh-huh," dubiously. "Mebbe it wouldn't be safe. The kid got drunk last night in the Lily of the Valley saloon, and he backed ag'in' the bar, with a gun in his hand, and recited some startlin' pedigrees. But nobody called him."

"Felt sorry for him, I suppose."

"Thasso?"

The sheriff squinted at Trainor.

"That kid took seven dollars away from Lonesome Hobbs day before yesterday, shootin' with a six-gun. I throwed the tin-cans for 'em m'self. Hobbs ain't so danged amachoor, y'betcha."

"Well, let him go ahead." Trainor shrugged his shoulders, as if to dismiss the subject.

"Oh, he'll go too far, that's a cinch," said the sheriff. "Kids always does. I wish that danged jury would make up their minds pretty soon. There's Cassidy's girl over in front of the hardware store now. I betcha she's lookin' for Ben Lanpher."

Trainor turned and squinted closely at her. She was about average height, with a thin oval face, as brown as her maternal ancestors, but showing little of the aboriginal blood. Her hair was dark and worn in two heavy braids, but her eyes were blue.

Her calico dress was well-made, even though a trifle gaudy in color, and she walked with the easy grace of a jungle-bred animal.

"Irish and Injun," muttered Trainor. "Hell, what a combination! A blue-eyed Injun. If she wanted a weapon and you showed her a brickbat and a scalpin' knife, which would she take?"

"That's a question," grinned the sheriff. "But she's a damn pretty girl, jist the same, Trainor."

"Yes, she's damn pretty."

"And she'll make a good wife for some man."

"Hm-m-m," mused Trainor. "I reckon she will."

Two cowboys were crossing the street and Trainor turned from looking at Lorna Cassidy to give them a sharp glance.

"Who are those fellers, Fleager?" he asked.

"One feller—the tall one—is named Hartley. I talked with him this mornin' at the feed corral. They rode in last night from the Enemas country."

"Goin' to stay here?"

"Lookin' for jobs, I reckon. The tall feller is a nice spoken sort of a jigger, but he made me feel like he was laughin' at me all the time. There ain't nothin' soft and tender about either of 'em."

"What did he say that made yuh feel he was laughin' at yuh?"

"Oh-h-h, well—nothin' much. He was tellin' about a feller that he knew who was so durned thin that his clothes wouldn't stay on him, and so he wore his union-suit on the outside. He said it sure looked awful, but gave him the full use of his two bands."

The sheriff hitched up his pants and belt and spat reflectively, while a grin flashed across Trainor's thin lips.

"Anyway," declared the sheriff, "I ain't goin' to try it. Mebbe we better go over and see if there's any news from the jury."

As they started across the street, Hashknife and Sleepy came out of the saloon and caught up with them. Hashknife spoke to the sheriff.

"You ain't puttin' on this kind of weather for our benefit, are yuh, pardner?"

"This ain't so hot," said the sheriff.

"No, it ain't exactly hot. I knowed a man once that was so danged thin that—"

"Your name's Hartley, ain't it?" interrupted the sheriff. "Shake hands with Mr. Trainor, of the Circle Cross."

Hashknife shook hands with Trainor and introduced Sleepy to both men.

"You two fellers just driftin' through?" queried Trainor casually.

Hashknife grinned and shook his head.

"Feller asked the same thing about a week ago. No-o-o, I wouldn't say that we're exactly driftin', Mr. Trainor."

"We're kinda lookin' for jobs," declared Sleepy. "We ain't askin' for work—for jobs."

Trainor laughed.

"I'm full-handed right now, or will be, as soon as that jury finds out what they're goin' to do. My foreman is on the jury, yuh see."

"Seems like they was havin' trouble decidin' the case, accordin' to what I can hear," observed Hashknife. "Old man Cassidy ain't very pop'lar, is he?"

"Not very," admitted Trainor. "I reckon they'll cinch him."

The sheriff shook his head and shifted his chew.

"Nossir, I don't think so. 'F they was goin' to cinch him they'd 'a' done it hours ago. Cow-juries don't work that-away."

"They sure don't," grinned Hashknife. "They're just as liable to bring in a verdict of arson ag'in' the judge as to settle the guilt or innocence of old man Cassidy."

"And still they're twelve men, good and true," grunted Trainor.

"Good and true don't mean that they've got any brains."

"Here comes 'Lonesome' Hobbs," said the sheriff, pointing down the street toward a short, fat, bow-legged individual, who was coming toward them as fast as his feet would carry him. As he drew near he removed his hat, exposing an almost totally bald head, which made him look like a very fat and very much overheated baby.

"Juj-jury's made up their dud-danged minds," he panted hoarsely. "Do yuh know where the juj-judge is, Fat?"

"He's over in the Lily of the Valley, I reckon. Better go over and roust him out, Lonesome."

"Uh-huh. I'll git 'm."

Lonesome bow-legged his way across the street, fanning himself with his hat, while Hashknife and Sleepy followed Trainor and the sheriff down to the dance-hall, which was used as a courtroom.

Lonesome's search for the judge had spread the news that the jury had reached a decision, and the court filled rapidly. Hashknife and Sleepy secured seats near the front of the room.

Seated just beyond them was Lorna Cassidy, and in a few minutes she was joined by a stout, white-haired man, carrying a mass of legal-looking papers.

"That's Mitchell, the Frisco lawyer," whispered a man near Hashknife. "I heard that young Lanpher hired him to defend old man Cassidy. I betcha it cost him some money."

A few minutes later the sheriff came in from the rear of the hall, and with him was Pinto Cassidy, a little, old, wizened character. Cassidy was typically Irish of face, and his steady glance at the audience seemed to carry a fighting challenge to any or all of them.

But his seamed old face softened as he looked at his daughter, and he smiled softly, patting her on the shoulder. They talked together for a moment and then Ben Lanpher came swaggering up the aisle to sit down beside her. He was flushed with drink, arrogant with the feeling that every one was against him, and looked defiantly at every one in the room.

The judge came in and stood beside his desk. He was an old man, white of hair, very dignified. For a moment he looked about the room and rapped sharply on his desk. The buzz of conversation ceased.

"Just to say to you," said the judge clearly, "that the court will brook no demonstration whatever. You will curb your feelings while within these walls."

He turned and sat down as the jury filed in. They were a tired-looking crew of men, stolid, some of them seemingly half-angry. They sat down in the jury-box and looked expectantly at the judge, who said—

"Gentlemen, have you reached a decision?"

A big, raw-boned cowman, the foreman of the jury, got to his feet slowly and faced the judge.

"We have not," he replied evenly, "and we can't. There's a damn fool among us that—" He looked meaningly at a hard-faced, squint-eyed cowboy on the end of the row—"that ain't got enough brains to grease a needle with. He's held us up for—well, all the time we've been in then, and we ask that you dismiss us."

The squint-eyed cowboy continued to study the opposite wall, paying no attention to the foreman's words. The judge cleared his throat raspingly.

"Then you find it impossible to reach a verdict?"

"Yeah, unless we want to foller that half-witted gopher's ideas and hang old man Cassidy, judge. If it wasn't murder to kill a feller like him, he'd 'a' been dead eleven times right now."

"And that's no damn lie," echoed a disgruntled member.

The judge sighed. He had been many years in cow-land and knew there would be no use to reprimand these men for such language in the court-room. They were all on the ragged edge, and the only thing he could do would be to dismiss them, which he did; thanking them for their efforts.

Ben Lanpher got to his feet and spoke directly to the judge:

"What about Cassidy? Does he get off now?"

The judge shook his head.

"No, I am sorry to say that he will have to stand trial before another jury."

"There's a hell of a lot of justice in that!" roared Ben angrily. "Eleven of 'em wanted to turn him loose, and just because one man—"

"Hang on to yourself, Lanpher!" snapped the sheriff, taking him by the arm. "You're in a courtroom—not a saloon."

"That's right," gritted the boy. "We might get justice in a saloon, but we can't get it here."

The sheriff turned and looked at the judge questioningly, but the judge shook his head sadly and turned back toward the rear door. The jury had got to their feet, and the sheriff crossed quickly to them and moved in close to the squint-eyed cause of their disgust.

"I'll walk out with yuh," said the sheriff.

"You better walk with him," grunted one of the jury meaningly."

"Yes, and you better stay with him," added Ben Lanpher.

The squint-eyed one glanced at Lanpher and the lines around his mouth twitched sharply, but he did not reply. Hashknife and Sleepy left the courtroom and went back to the street, where men were discussing the trial.

A cowboy, somewhat the worse for liquor, came up to them.

"Kinda looks like they was goin' to have a hard time convictin' old Cassidy," he observed. "I'll betcha that jury had a hell of a time. But you mark my word, this ain't all settled yet."

"No?" queried Hashknife. "How's that, pardner?"

"Huh! Lemme tell yuh somethin'. That squint-eyed 'Smoky' Cole'll make 'em pay for what they said about him, y'betcha. He's plumb salty, he is. I sabe that jasper. Any time yuh think yo're runnin' a blazer on that son-of-a-gun, yo're foolin' yourself, thasall."

"Bad, is he?" queried Hashknife.

"I'll nod when yuh ask me that," grinned the cowboy.

"You knowed him a long time—before he came here?"

The cowboy sobered a trifle and hitched up his belt.

"Tell yuh what I'll do, I'll buy a drink."

"Who does Smoky Cole work for?" asked Sleepy.

"He's foreman of the Circle Cross. Works for Trainor. I'm named Edwards, but folks calls me 'Bility.'"

"Is that yore real name, or is it short for Ability."

"Hell, I dunno. Yuh see—"

He grinned and spilled half a sack of tobacco past his cigaret paper.

"Yuh see, I been with the Flyin' M f'r a long time, and one time some fellers was thinkin' about buyin' old man Shappee out. They was arguin' about things, when I comes up to see the old man, and one of 'em says—

"'Is this one of yore assets?'

"And old man Shappee says:

"'Hell, no! That feller is a liability.'"

The cowboy laughed and spilled the rest of his tobacco.

"Do yuh know what it means?" asked Hashknife.

"Hell, no! And I don't care. Let's go. It got me a name."

They went into the Lily of the Valley, which was the biggest saloon in the town, and found Trainor at the bar, talking with Lonesome Hobbs. The place was fairly well-filled and the games of chance were being well-patronized.

They accepted of Bility's hospitality and while they were drinking, Ben Lanpher came in. He drank two big drinks of raw liquor before he paid any attention to those at the bar. His eyes were red from liquor and his jaw sagged listlessly.

Hashknife studied him closely and decided that Bennie Lanpher had the makings of a bad-man. He had evidently practised with a six-gun until he had an exalted idea of his own ability, and plenty of liquor had made him careless.

Ben turned and looked at Hashknife, who smiled softly. Bennie was in no mood to have any one smile at him, and his weak jaw immediately assumed a belligerent angle.

"See anythin' funny about me?" he grunted.

Hashknife ignored the question and turned back facing the bar. But Ben was not to be denied. Something seemed to tell him that this tall cowpuncher had smiled at him—possibly laughed at him.

He shoved away from the bar and stepped in behind Hashknife.

"See anythin' funny about me?" he asked.

Hashknife turned lazily and looked him straight in the eyes.

"Yeah, I see a lot of funny things about yuh, young feller. If they wasn't also awful sad, I'd laugh like—"

"Is—that—so?" Lanpher spaced his words widely and his right hand eased back toward his holster.

"In the first place," continued Hashknife, "yo're too young to drink so much liquor. First thing yuh know you'll quit growin' and always look like a half-baked kid. You ain't got brain enough to see that yo're headin' plumb into trouble—mebbe a rope. Them is some of the reasons why I ain't laughin' at yuh."

Lanpher laughed mockingly, loudly and then his teeth fairly snapped. The room had gone quiet and every one had heard what Hashknife had said, although he had spoken quietly.

"Take it kinda easy," advised Hashknife. "I'm a stranger to you and we ain't got no quarrel."

"Backin' up, eh?" snarled Lanpher. "Next time you laugh at a man, you'll find out who he is first."

Lanpher's hand was on the butt of his gun and his body tensed forward, expecting that Hashknife would accept his challenge. But Hashknife's eyes squinted just past Lanpher's head and his left eyelid drew down quickly in a deliberate wink.

Lanpher's head twisted as quick as a flash; thinking that there was danger right behind him, and before he could turn back Hashknife's left hand had caught him by the right wrist, while Hashknife's open right hand splatted against the side of his jaw, throwing him off his balance and placing him powerless to do anything, except swear.

And Lanpher did plenty of the latter. Hashknife held him helpless, while the crowd moved in close to enjoy the sight.

"Yuh got a lot of things to learn before yuh can be a honest-to-gosh bad-man," explained Hashknife. "And one of 'em is to never turn yore head."

"Lemme go!" wailed Lanpher.

"All right, I'll let yuh go," agreed Hashknife, "but you've got to agree to one thing."

"All right, damn yuh. What is it?"

"As soon as yuh get yore balance, we'll both start shootin'."

The crowd behind Lanpher parted with great alacrity.

But Lanpher did not care for the conditions. Hashknife flung him away and Lanpher staggered into a card-table before he regained his balance. Then he went straight out of the door, without looking back.

"That's tamin' 'em," declared Trainor, who had been an interested observer. "It was just what he needed, Hartley. I'll buy a drink."

The crowd went back to their games, but the incident was not forgotten. Hashknife was a stranger, which was worthy of notice in Wolf Wells, where few strangers ever came, and he had demonstrated that he was able to take care of himself in a way that appealed to the range folk.

"I wish I had a job for you fellers," said Trainer, as they leaned on the bar, "but I'm plumb filled up right now."

"We ain't exactly dependent on a job right now," explained Hashknife, "but a feller don't like to go broke before he lands a job. Who'd be a good rancher to see about a job?"

"I dunno. Yuh might see old man Shappee. He owns the Flyin' M, but I suppose he's got a full crew."

"How much of a crew do you have, Trainor?"

"I'm only hirin' three men now. Nothin' much to do this time of the year, except to kinda watch the waterholes. We're break-in' a few horses, too. Usually I have five or six men. I had kinda bad luck lately. Mebbe yuh heard about two of my men gettin' shot."

"Got shot?" Hashknife shook his head. "We ain't been here long enough to hear much gossip. Was it for the killin' of one of them that Cassidy is bein' tried?"

"Yeah, the last one. Mebbe he killed the first one, I dunno."

"He don't look like a killer." This from Sleepy.

"No, he don't, but he's meaner than a snake."

"Just in what way?" Hashknife was curious, and Trainor glanced quickly at him.

"Oh, just mean. He said he'd shoot the first Circle Cross man he found on the Tomahawk."

Hashknife grinned.

"He must have a grudge ag'in' yore outfit, Trainor."

Trainor grunted an unintelligible reply and turned as some one called his name. It was an undersized cowboy, with a limp cigaret glued to his protruding underlip.

"You seen Whitey Anderson?" he asked.

"Not today," replied Trainor.

"He was lookin' for yuh about fifteen minutes ago."

"All right, Shorty."

Trainor accepted another drink and left the saloon.

"Who's Anderson?" asked Hashknife of the bartender.

"Depot agent."

CHAPTER III

THEY drifted outside and found Lonesome Hobbs sitting on a hitch-rack. How he ever got himself up that high was a mystery, but he was up there. He nodded to Hashknife and Sleepy and slid over to give them room.

"I seen yuh have yore fuss with young Lanpher," he said huskily. "Bub-by gosh, he needed a jolt. How'd yuh ever think up that winkin' idea?"

"Used my head," grinned Hashknife.

"That's it," nodded Lonesome. "Feller's got to use his brains—if he's gug-got any. I can think of the best doggone schemes, but I forget 'em right when I need 'em bad. Feller told me a good scheme once. Said to step hard on a feller's feet, when yo're fightin' him and he'll fall down. I tried it—once."

"Didn't it work?" asked Sleepy.

"Not fer me, it didn't. I reckon that was only part of the trick; the rest of it was to keep the other feller from knockin' the hell out of yuh until yuh could fuf-find his feet. Anyway, that's how she 'pears to me."

They were laughing as Trainor came up to the rack and untied his roan horse.

"Goin' home?" asked Hashknife.

"Yeah. Wish I had a job for you two. Hope you get one."

"Much obliged," grinned Hashknife. "We'll swindle somebody out of a few month's wages. Adios."

"Seems like a right nice sort of a feller," observed Hashknife, as Trainor rode away.

"Who, Trainor? Best there is, y'betcha. Hanged good cowman, top-notch puncher and reliable as—"

"Which is some reliability," agreed Hashknife. "We'd kinda like to work for him."

"Well, I dunno whether I would or not." Lonesome pursed his lips thoughtfully. "I'm kinda superstitious, don'tcha know it? I figgers that things happens three times before they quits. There's been two of the Circle Cross punchers killed lately. They was leaded considerable, too.

"Figgerin' the way I do, there's another one to go. It don't always work out that-away, of course, bub-but I ain't the kind of a jasper that goes dead ag'in' my own hunches."

"Why do yuh reckon they was killed?" queried Sleepy.

"Why." Lonesome leaned his elbows on his knees and shook his head. "I ain't prepared to say."

"Any idea who killed 'em?"

"Well, they're tryin' old Cassidy for the last one."

"Where is Cassidy's ranch?" asked Hashknife.

Lonesome jerked his thumb in a northerly direction.

"Out thataway. Yuh take the main road out there, and a little over two miles she folks, but don't take the right-hand fork, 'cause that goes to the Circle Cross. Keep on goin' about a quarter-mile and take the left-hand road.

"It's about seven miles to the Tomahawk, and about five to the Circle Cross. I'd keep plumb away from the Tomahawk, if I was you. They ain't a danged bit friendly."

"But Cassidy is where he can't hurt anybody."

"No, he can't, but there's young Lanpher livin' there, and Jimmy Droop-drawers."

Hashknife laughed outright.

"For gosh sake, what a name!"

"He's a half-breed," grinned Lonesome, "and that name fits him like a plaster. Jimmy was absent the day they was passin' around the brains, but he sure can shoot."

"You got kind of a sweet lot of folks around here," observed Hashknife. "Looks to me like Wolf Wells had enough gunmen to hold up the reputation of a bigger place."

"Aw, we ain't botherin' with gunmen." Lonesome spat dryly and shook his head. "We ain't afraid of nothin' we can see, y'betcha. It's the things we can't see that gits under our hides."

"Such as what?" asked Hashknife.

"Cows that evaporate, for instance."

Hashknife and Sleepy looked closely at Lonesome, but his face was deadly serious.

"Well," said Hashknife slowly. "I've heard of evaporated milk. Mebbe that's where it come from, Lonesome."

"Mum-mebbe," dubiously. "Anyway, it ain't a fav'rite subject with me, gents. I reckon I'll be goin' back to the office. You ain't found no jobs yet?"

He almost fell off the hitch-rack, without waiting for an answer, recovered his hat, which rolled under a horse, and bow-legged his way across the street.

Sleepy grinned and looked at Hashknife. "What do you think of things, Hashknife?"

"Well, it's too danged early in the game to make any remarks, but I'll say there's a lot of folks around here that might start shootin' any time.

"I don't think a lot of old man Lanpher's offspring, but I do like his pardner. Trainor seems like a regular he-man. The sheriff has only one thing to recommend him, and that is the fact he's so danged thin that nobody could hit him with anythin' bigger than a .22 rifle.

"Lonesome Hobbs is all right. Old man Cassidy might 'a' killed that puncher, but I have my doubts. His girl is danged pretty, and William Lanpher might be danged well honored to think that she'd look at his slack-headed son. Outside of that, I'm hungry. Let's go and eat."

"All right," agreed Sleepy. "I kinda feel that we're goin' to like Wolf Wells. It kinda reminds me of the old Wilier Crick outfit, Hashknife. Everybody suspicious of everybody else. I sure hope they don't suspicion us."

"They will, if we don't get a job, Sleepy."

As they crossed the street, Ben Lanpher, Cassidy's squaw and Lorna Cassidy were getting into a fight wagon. Lanpher saw them, but did not look up as they passed. The girl gave them a keen glance and the two cowboys lifted their hats. As they went into a restaurant, Hashknife looked back and the girl had turned her head and was watching them.

"I hope she knows us next time she sees us," said Sleepy, grinning.

"I hope they all do," replied Hashknife. "I'd hate to be mistaken for some of the boys from the Circle Cross."

* * * *

The Tomahawk was a typical squaw-man's ranch. There was little semblance of order in the locations of the ranch-house, barns or corrals, and the buildings looked as if they might collapse in the next breeze.

The weather-beaten ranch-house, a low, rambling affair, was sway-backed from old age and the weight of many snows, and the barn stood, as a cowboy might express it, kinda antegodlin' to everythin'. The corral fences were lopsided and badly in need of repair.

A few mongrel chickens strayed around the littered front yard of the ranch-house, clucking wildly after the winged grasshoppers; a family of magpies chattered in the cottonwoods behind the barn, while down in a corral a hungry calf bawled loudly.

It was the day following the dimissal of the jury. In the long living-room Ben Lanpher humped over in a dilapidated rocking-chair, staring moodily at a crumpled envelope. His hair was matted, his face unshaven and his clothes bore evidence that he had slept in them—and not on a bed.

Lorna Cassidy leaned against the side of the adobe fireplace, looking with troubled eyes at Lanpher, while near her the squat figure of Mrs. Cassidy was seated on a low stool. At the far end of the room, sitting on the floor, with his knees drawn up to his chin, was the half-breed cowboy, known by the unlovely title of Jimmy Droop-drawers.

Jimmy was a typical half-breed, in which the Indian blood seemed to predominate strongly. His lower lip was thick and pendulous, his eyes mere slits above his high cheek-bones, and his garb, with the exception of his high-heeled boots, badly run-over at the heels, was entirely aboriginal. It was plainly evident that his beaded-blanket pants had not been made by a tailor, because the seat was entirely too commodious—which accounted for his cognomen.

Ben Lanpher crumpled the letter in his hand and got to his feet.

"Well—" He tried to laugh, but it was only a grimace. "Well, that settles the cat-hop, I suppose. The old man has cut off my credit—told me that I could have no more of his money."

He turned his head and looked at Lorna.

"Well, why don't somebody say something? I'm too damn dry even to curse him."

"There is nothing to say," said Lorna softly.

"Ain't there?" Ben laughed hoarsely. "It means that we won't be able to hire a lawyer for the next trial. I'm broke."

"Why need lawyer?" asked Mrs. Cassidy. "My man never kill cowboy. Only one man think so."

"That damn Smoky Cole!" snapped Ben. "I'll fill him so full of holes that he'll—"

"And who will pay for the lawyer to keep you from hanging?" asked Lorna quickly.

"You don't need a lawyer when you kill a man in self-defense."

"Yo' look out," advised Jimmy thickly. "Cole bad man with a gun. Mebbe yo' need doctor—not lawyer."

"Too much talk about kill," said the stolid old squaw, as she slowly filled a pipe with plug tobacco. "No good to talk."

"Tha's jus' right," nodded Jimmy. "Old Minnie know. Big talk, small medicine."

"Who were those two men who passed, when we were ready to leave Wolf Wells yesterday?" asked Lorna.

"Them two?" Ben took a half-filled bottle from his hip pocket and reached for a tin cup on the table.

"I dunno who they are. Couple of smart cowpunchers, I guess."

"Ben, why don't you go back to your home?"

"Huh?"

Ben took the cup away from his lips and stared at her.

"Why don't I go home?"

"Yes—back to your people."

Ben laughed harshly.

"Why should I go back to them?"

"They are your people. You don't belong here. They would be glad to have you come back."

"Whatcha talkin' about, Lorna?"

Lanpher was half-angry, as he got to his feet and walked over to her.

"I told yuh I'd stay here and see that the old man was cleared. Dad wanted me to stay with the Circle Cross, but me and Trainor couldn't get along. He treated me like I was a kid. Told me not to come over here. Said that you was just a damn Injun, and that your father would shoot me if I came on the Tomahawk ranch."

Lorna turned and stared out of the window, her lips shut tight, as if to hold back a flood of bitterness. Then—

"Well, I suppose he was right, Ben."

"What do we care?" laughed Ben hoarsely. "If I want to marry an Injun, that's my business, ain't it?"

Lorna shook her head.

"No, you are just foolish, I think. You go back to your people and forget everybody in the Ghost Hills."

"Not by a damn sight! When I go back to California—to Frisco, you are going with me, Lorna."

The old squaw took her pipe slowly from her lips and looked up at Ben.

"You are very big damn fool, I think," she declared.

"Is that so?"

Ben turned to the old squaw.

"Mebbe you'd have somethin' to say about it?"

She nodded slowly and began puffing on her pipe.

Ben shrugged his shoulders and poured himself another drink. He had imbibed so much liquor during the last two weeks that his system shrieked for more.

"Why don't you quit drinking?" asked Lorna. "When you came here you did not drink."

"Lot of things I didn't do then."

Ben wiped his mouth with the back of his hand and laughed uncertainly, as he looked closely at his almost depleted flask.

"I've got to go to town and get more hooch."

"What will you do when your money is all gone?"

"Do?"

Ben laughed and picked up his hat.

"Rob a bank, I guess. Maybe I'll join the Ghost Hills gang. By God, I'll bet they'd take me in."

He turned and walked out of the door, staggering slightly, as he clumped off the porch and headed for the barn. Jimmy, the half-breed, walked to the door where he leaned lazily against the sill, puffing on his cigaret.

The old squaw did not turn her bead as Ben went out, but continued to puff at her pipe, while Lorna moved from the fireplace and stood beside the table, her shapely fingers picking at the cloth.

"Just a damn Injun," she said softly, sadly. "Just that and nothing more. Am I any different or worse than other girls?"

The squaw knocked the dottle from her pipe and got clumsily to her feet, which were shod in buckskin.

"You good girl, Lorna. Good Injun just as good as white people."

"You damn right!" agreed Jimmy from the doorway. "You jus' right, Lorna. To hell with Trainor."

Jimmy turned away from the door and came back toward them.

"Ben gone to town," he announced, and added. "Too much whisky no good."

He squatted at the fireplace and started to roll another cigaret, but his trained ears heard a sound outside and he arose swiftly and his hand swung back to jerk his revolver holster into position.

Came the scrape of a footstep on the narrow porch and Jim Trainor's voice called—

"Anybody home?"

"Somebody home," replied Jimmy huskily. He was just a trifle afraid of the big man from the Circle Cross.

Trainor's huge frame fairly blocked the door as he came in from the porch. Lorna looked straight at him, but the old squaw, after the manner of her kind, paid him no heed. Jimmy watched him closely.

"Hello, Lorna," grinned Trainor, "I got to wonderin' how you folks were gettin' along so I came over to see. Where's Ben Lanpher?"

"He go to town," said Jimmy. "Go jus' now."

"Gone down to get drunk again, I suppose."

Trainor sat down in the rocking-chair and threw his hat on the table. He seemed entirely at home, even though his welcome had not been any too cordial.

"Why do you come here?" asked Lorna.

"Why?" Trainor laughed shortly. "I told you I wanted to see how you were all getting along, Lorna."

"That should not take long to find out, Mr. Trainor."

"No, I guess that's a fact. Too bad about that jury."

"Too damn bad," corrected Jimmy, and was immediately sorry he had spoken.

Trainor turned and looked straight at him.

"When I speak to you, I'll call you by name."

Jimmy swallowed with difficulty and sidled toward the door. He was not of a belligerent disposition and he greatly respected Trainor's fighting ability. At the doorway he turned and fired a parting shot.

"Next time jury agree, mebbe. You know what Pinto Cassidy said about Circle Cross men."

And then Jimmy Droop-drawers faded out of sight. Trainor's face went black for a moment, and the ghost of a smile flitted across the old squaw's face, but Trainor passed it off with a laugh.

"I hope they do agree," he laughed, "and I don't think that Pinto Cassidy will be so hasty next time."

"You believe my father killed him?"

Lorna leaned across the table and looked Trainor square in the eyes.

"Well—" Trainor looked away and rubbed his chin with the ball of his right thumb. "Well, I hope not, Lorna. But if he did he was only making good his threat. Ed Meeker had no business coming over here. He knew what Cassidy had said."

"Who killed the other man—Lloyd Hansen? He wasn't found on the Tomahawk."

"I don't know who killed him. But your father ain't accused of that killin'."

"Why was he killed?" demanded Lorna.

"Why?" Trainor shrugged his shoulders. "Who knows. But that does not interest me. Did Ben get a letter from his father lately?"

Lorna turned away from the table and sat down near the old squaw.

"I know nothing about Ben's mail," she replied.

Trainor smiled.

"He's sayin' that he's goin' to marry you, Lorna."

"I have no strings on his tongue," indifferently.

"I thought he was lyin'," smiled Trainor. "His father wrote me that he had sent word to Ben that his money supply was cut off. It's about time, I reckon."

"Ben is a fool," continued Trainor, when Lorna ignored his statement. "His father is wealthy and can give him everything he would want. He can marry a white girl and live in a fine house; so why should he stay around here?"

"And marry a damn Injun," added Lorna.

Trainor looked keenly at her. He remembered saying those same words to Ben, and wondered if he had told her.

"Well, you know how city folks look at Indians, Lorna. You don't look like an Injun. If I didn't know different, I'd never know that you had a drop of Indian blood in yuh."

"What have the Indians ever done to make a white man look down upon their blood?" asked Lorna hoarsely. "They only fought for what had belonged to them for many years. It was not that they wanted to win more, but to keep what they already owned.

"I know. I have read history in school. I have read many tales of the Indian—written by men who knew only the one half of the tale—the white half. The Indian fought in his own way—the only way he knew.

"The Indian was lazy, because that was his disposition, but the squaw was not lazy. And the Indian was honest and sober until the white man—that superior race—came to ruin his morals and soul. He taught the Indian to lie, steal and drink. Perhaps—" Lorna turned away scornfully—"it will take many more years to bring the Indian up to the standard which the white man started to teach him many years ago."

Trainor laughed loudly and slapped his thigh.

"Lorna, when you turn loose, I wonder if you've got any white blood in yuh."

"I am never ashamed of Indian blood," she retorted, "but there are times when I am ashamed of my white blood."

"All right," grinned Trainor. "I don't blame yuh. Let's drop the subject. I never like to argue with a lady."

"Bad business," grunted the old squaw.

"That's right, Minnie," agreed Trainor, laughing. "Anyway, I like Lorna too well to argue with her."

He got to his feet and picked up his hat.

"I'm going to run in real often," he stated. "Cassidy won't get another trial before the next term of court, and that'll be three months from now. You'll probably be needing a little help before he can get cleared, and I want yuh to understand that the Circle Cross is willing to help yuh in any way we can."

"Good!" grunted the old squaw.

But Lorna did not express any thanks for his offer. He looked keenly at her before he turned toward the door. She gave him a side-long glance as he went out through the door, but it was not a look of gratitude.

She heard him gallop away, going back toward the Circle Cross, and then she sat down beside the table. The old squaw had put away her pipe and was softly crooning a Sioux cradle-song, a chanting, tuneless thing that recited the superiority of the Sioux papoose over anything else on earth. It was one of the first things Lorna remembered, but she shuddered just now. It seemed so foolish to think that the Indian could be superior.

"Perhaps," she told herself, "it is the white blood that rises above the red and makes me dislike Indian songs."

The squaw finished the song and started all over again. Lorna got to her feet and walked to the door, as if to get away from the song, and as she looked out into the sunlight, two riders, the two men who had lifted their hats to her in Wolf Wells, were riding up to the house.

Jimmy, the half-breed, was working around one of the corrals, but when he saw the two men he came up toward the house. Hash-knife and Sleepy took off their hats and spoke to Lorna pleasantly.

"We was just ridin' around, ma'am, and thought mebbe we could get a drink of water," explained Hashknife, "We tried to take a drink out of the little creek below here, but it was a little too bitter with alkali."

"We have plenty of water," replied the girl, and turned to the half-breed.

"Jimmy, will you get some water from the well? These men want a drink." Jimmy squinted at the two cowboys for a moment before he turned and went around the house. Hashknife and Sleepy dismounted and came up to the steps, just as Mrs. Cassidy came over to the door.

"Hello, mother," smiled Hashknife. "How are you today?"

The old squaw smiled broadly at the title and nodded pleasantly. Hashknife turned to Lorna.

"This is the Tomahawk ranch, ain't it?" he asked.

"Yes."

"Uh-huh. Yuh see, I wasn't sure. Somebody told us that we'd likely get shot if we came here, but we don't believe everythin' we hear."

Lorna smiled, but there was little happiness in it.

"I am glad you did not believe," she replied. "We have never killed any one."

"Sure yuh ain't," agreed Sleepy heartily. "I can jist look at you and see that yuh never. Gosh dang it, some folks sure do get things twisted."

Hashknife squinted sidewise at Sleepy and a grin spread his lips. Sleepy saw the grin and shuffled his feet nervously.

"Well," he said defensively, "can't you, Hashknife?"

"I never disputed yuh, cowboy," grinned Hashknife.

Jimmy came around the corner with a bucket of water and the two cowboys quenched their thirst.

"Best water I ever drank," declared Sleepy. "Never knowed that water could taste so danged good. Betcha I'll be ridin' this way real of ten f'r my drinks. Don'tcha know." Sleepy was almost confidential. "I wonder why men drink strong liquor, when water tastes so good."

"Now, little Dew-drop, don't get so enthusiastic," advised Hashknife seriously, and then to Lorna—

"He's the same way over everythin, ma'am."

"He likes water," said the old squaw.

"Under bridges," admitted Hashknife. "Sleepy—say, I plumb forgot to introduce us. I'm Hashknife Hartley and this here water-soaked pardner of mine is named Sleepy Stevens."

"I am Lorna Cassidy," said the girl, "and this is my mother, Mrs. Cassidy."

"We're sure pleased to meetcha," said Sleepy, bowing gracefully, but kicking over the water-bucket at the same time.

"You've gotta watch him all the time," explained Hashknife, as Sleepy hastened to right the bucket. "He'll get his feet right into anythin' that's got water in it."

Sleepy stood up, a grin on his flushed face. Lorna was laughing and a wide grin overspread the old squaw's face. Jimmy, the half-breed stepped in and held out his hand to Hashknife.

"I'm Jimmy," he said. "Nobody speak my name."

Hashknife and Sleepy shook hands solemnly with him.

"You'll excuse me, won't yuh Jimmy?" asked Hashknife, "and we both thank yuh for the water."

Jimmy grinned.

"Plenty water. You want more?"

"No, thank yuh, Jimmy. If there was any more water around here, I'd have to get a canoe for Sleepy. He can't swim a lick."

Jimmy grunted and went away with the bucket. He had no sense of humor, but he instinctively liked these two cowpunchers. Perhaps it was because they shook hands with him and treated him as an equal.

"My man in jail," said Mrs. Cassidy, as if explaining his absence. "Can't get out. Too damn much law."

"Yeah, I reckon that's right, mother," said Hashknife, "but he'll get out."

"Won't you come in?" asked Lorna. "It is cool in the house."

"Betcha we will," agreed Sleepy quickly. "I'm about fried to a cinder."

Jimmy followed them into the house and sat down against the wall.

"Ben Lanpher lives here, don't he?" asked Hashknife.

"He has been staying here," corrected Lorna. "Do you know him?"

"He was pointed out to me, and they said he was livin' here."

"Too much whisky," grunted the old squaw.

Hashknife smiled and rolled a cigaret. He had been afraid to ask questions in Wolf Wells for fear that some one might find out that he and Sleepy were investigating the rustling situation.

"You folks been losin' any cattle?" he asked.

Lorna nodded quickly.

"Yes, I think so. Dad insists that we have. He told everybody that he was losing cattle, and two days after that we found a card pinned to the front door. It had been written with a pencil and told us to keep our mouths shut or something worse than loss of cattle would come to us."

"Don't talk about it," advised Jimmy warningly.

Hashknife and Sleepy exchanged glances. They knew now why there was no talk about the rustlers. It was the fear of the unknown that had shut the lips of the cattlemen. It was a condition that would make every man suspect his neighbor.

"Where do the cattle go?" asked Hashknife. "You've got to have a market for stolen stock. Is there any way out of here, except by railroad, where cattle could have been sent?"

Lorna shook her head.

"I can't talk about it with you," she said. "You are strangers to us, and for all we know you may belong to the Ghost Hills gang. Every one is afraid around here. Two men have already been killed and I think they were killed by the rustlers, but we have no proofs."

"Ghost Hills gang, eh?" said Hashknife thoughtfully. "Have they ever been seen by any one?"

"No seeum," grunted the old squaw.

"Sort of fantom riders, eh?" grinned Sleepy. "I dunno whether we want jobs in this range or not, Hashknife. I'm kinda spooky m'self."

"Does kinda make a feller feel creepy," admitted Hashknife seriously, "and I don't blame you folks for not talkin' too much. I don't suppose the sheriff is spendin' much time tryin' to round 'em up."

"He stay home," grunted Jimmy. "Sheriff smart man."

Hashknife laughed softly and picked up his hat.

"Well, folks, I reckon we'll drift along. Can we cut straight across the hills to Wolf Wells?"

"Yeah," grunted Jimmy. "No fence, no trail. Not so long as road."

Lorna followed them to the door and watched them mount.

"Will you come again?" she asked, just a trifle wistfully.

"Unless the ghost riders plug me first," said Sleepy quickly.

"She meant both of us," grinned Hashknife, as they rode away. "Sleepy, you sure do lose what little sense yuh got when yuh see a pretty girl."

"Well, by golly, she sure is a pretty girl, Hashknife. She's got Lanpher's daughter beat four ways from the jack."

Hashknife turned in his saddle and looked keenly at Sleepy, who was looking back toward the Tomahawk ranch-house. Sleepy turned and encountered Hashknife's gaze.

"Rope's draggin' ag'in, Sleepy," warned Hashknife.

"Lemme alone, will yuh?" snapped Sleepy, spurring his horse ahead and up the brushy slope.

"There's some nice lookin' girls in the city," said Hashknife, quoting what Sleepy had said the night he had met Miss Lanpher.

But Sleepy only grunted. He and Hashknife had been partners for years, riding the ranges from Alberta to Mexico, and both were still heart and fancy free. Neither of them had ever been willing to marry and settle down. No range had ever been home to them for more than a few months at a time, and neither of them was young.

Both of them bore scars of conflict, and behind them were greater scars, which they had left in payment of injustice to others. They did not seek trouble, but, as Hashknife had said:

"There's an antidote for every kind of poison, Sleepy. Some of it ain't nothin' more than salt-water or soapsuds, but it does the trick. Poison is poison, whether it's somethin' yuh get out of a bottle or somethin' that grows in yore soul.

"When me and you first started hornin' into dirty deals, I figured we was professional trouble-shooters, but I've come to the conclusion that the good Lord intended us as an antidote for range poison. And we've sure cured a lot of hard cases."

"And never profited thereby," reminded Sleepy.

"No-o-o, but yuh never heard of soapsuds and salt-water yelpin' for pay. We're just antidotes, thasall."

Sleepy had a habit of falling in love at first sight, but it never went beyond that. Both of them realized that the marriage of one would mean the end of their adventures, and they were not ready to lead a peaceful life.

CHAPTER IV

FAT FLEAGER was putting in a bad afternoon. It was bad enough to have Smoky Cole in town, drunk. Smoky had been drinking alone since the jury had been discharged, and he was beginning to move around, as, if defying the whole world.

He had imbibed raw whisky for twenty-four hours, and was still on his feet. Not only was he on his feet, but he was fairly steady on them. His eye was bloodshot, but not at all bleary.

Fleager had observed Smoky Cole closely, waiting for him to run into some of the folks who had denounced him in the courtroom. Then came Ben Lanpher to add to the slat-like sheriff's troubles. Ben was nearly drunk when he reached town, and he lost no time in bracing his chest against the Lily of the Valley bar and filling his interior with fighting liquor.

Fat lost no time in hot-footing it back to the office and waking Lonesome Hobbs out of his mid-day siesta.

"Nouk," grunted Lonesome. "To hell with 'em both. Let 'em git at each other, Fat."

"But me and you have sworn to uphold the law," wailed the sheriff. "We've gotta do it, Lonesome."

"I'll hold her up," agreed Lonesome, getting off the bunk, adjusting his hat and selecting a sawed-off shotgun from the gun-rack.

"Where's all them buckshot shells, Fat?"

"Now whatcha goin' to do?"

"Shoot the hell out of both of 'em. It's gettin' so a fuf-feller can't even sleep around here. Where's the shells?"

"Aw-w-w, go lay down!" wailed the sheriff. "You ain't no help to me, Lonesome. You're either as lazy as the devil, or as bloodthirsty as a cannibal. I hired yuh as a deputy and all I got was a drawback."

"Well, whatcha want me to do?" grunted Lonesome. "I only know how to do two things real well—sleep and shoot. You woke me up, darn yuh, and now yuh won't let me know where them shells are. You ain't noways consistent."

"Yuh might use a little brains!" snapped the sheriff.

"If I had brains—" The cot creaked raspingly, as Lonesome stretched himself out again— "If I had brains I'd never live in Wolf Wells, I'll tell yuh that, Fat Fleager. Anyway, it ain't no job for a fat man, this ain't. All you've got to do is stand sideways and nobody can hit yuh. With me—"

Lonesome lifted his head and looked toward the door, but the sheriff had gone, and Lonesome did not finish his sentence.

Then he groaned dismally, got off the cot and buckled on his belt. He was in no mood to be trifled with now. It was his usual siesta time, and he meant to make it worth losing sleep over.

With Ben Lanpher in the Lily of the Valley, and Smoky Cole in the Antelope saloon, the sheriff planted himself between the two, which were half-a-block apart, and made a resolution that they—Ben and Smoky—must be kept apart.

The fact that one of them did not know the other was in town helped the sheriff considerably. Lonesome looked witheringly upon the watchful sheriff and went into the Lily of the Valley, where he found Ben Lanpher, standing with his shoulder-blades sort of hooked over the top of the bar, while he considered things of importance.

Lonesome Hobbs was no diplomat. He knew that Ben was just drunk enough to pick trouble. His bleary eye and the belligerent angle of his sombrero proclaimed to Lonesome that Bennie was contemplating starting something.

Lonesome walked up to the bar beside Ben, as if to buy a drink, turned swiftly and kicked Bennie's feet from under him. And while Bennie was going down in a sitting position, Lonesome uppercut him with a right fist, which landed Bennie into dreamland.

Then, while everything in the saloon suspended operations to watch him, Lonesome removed Bennie's gun, flipped out the cartridges and replaced the gun.

"And that's some sudden!" exclaimed the bartender.

"Dud-danged right," admitted Lonesome, and to the crowd—

"When he wakes up, you tell him to high-tail it out of town, 'cause I'm comin' back to make both sides of his face match up."

Then Lonesome went out of there, walking stiff-legged, and headed for the Antelope. The sheriff was still planted in the same spot, but Lonesome walked past him, as if the sheriff was a stranger. He spoke to Lonesome, but got no reply.

Lonesome went into the Antelope and found Smoky in a poker-game. Or rather, Smoky was half-in and half-out of the game. He was standing up, leaning across the table and talking in uncertain and very profane terms over what he declared to be a deliberate attempt to swindle him out of a pot.

Smoky was just drunk enough to be vile in his language, and dangerous withal. He was standing up in front of his chair when Lonesome's right hand hooked into his gaudy muffler, and a moment later he went over backward, taking the chair with him, and landed on the back of his head with a thud.

It knocked all the fight out of Smoky, and his mind was a blank during the time that Lonesome removed his gun and took out the cartridges. Smoky had no friends in the place to assist him, and those present seemed to get a lot of fun out of the incident.

"Tell him to rattle his hocks out of town," said Lonesome. "He's been makin' himself ob-obnoxious around here, and I'll be watchin' the front door for Ids goin'. Me and the sheriff is plumb tired of bein' annoyed."

Lonesome went out of the door and crossed the street toward the office, without looking at the sheriff, who was still holding forth between the two saloons. Lonesome went into the office and planted himself near the front window, after placing the sawed-off shotgun handy.

It was several minutes later that Ben Lanpher came to the door of the Lily of the Valley. His right hand caressed the side of his head and he seemed undecided as to what he intended doing. He took stock of the fact that the sheriff was between him and the Antelope saloon, but started walking toward him.

About this time Smoky Cole staggered out of the Antelope, his hat in his hand. He was also a trifle erratic in his movements, and perhaps a bit near-sighted after the bump on his head, because he too started toward the sheriff.

There was nothing for the sheriff to do but to move away from between them, which he did and did quickly.

"Don'tcha start nothin'!" he yelled. "Don'tcha—"

But his warning was wasted. The two belligerents had recognized each other. For a moment they hesitated, then two hands reached for two guns. Smoky was the faster of the two. His gun was out before Ben had started his draw, but the hammer fell upon an empty cylinder.

Swiftly his thumb hooked the hammer, and again the dull click of a dead cylinder. Ben's gun was leveled now, but his efforts were as unavailing as were Smoky's. But Smoky did not hear the click of Ben's gun, because Smoky was going away as fast as his legs would carry him.

Ben did not pay any attention to Smoky's going, because a quick glance told him that his gun was empty, and he turned to run the other way. Lonesome whooped with glee and fell backward on the cot, while the sheriff, after a glance in either direction, hurried across to the office.

Lonesome sat up and looked at the sheriff, his eyes filled with tears. The sheriff was a trifle pale and his lips worked soundlessly.

"What's the matter with you?" choked Lonesome.

"Thank the Lord!" exclaimed the sheriff. "I—I'm glad to hear your voice, Lonesome. I thought I had lost my hearin'. Them two guns—"

"Were empty," finished Lonesome. "Ha, ha, ha, ha! They never thought to look at 'em, and nobody told that I took out the shells."

"You took 'em out?"

"Yeah, I took 'em out," laughed Lonesome, and then told the sheriff what he had done to both men.

The sheriff went to the door and looked into the street. Ben Lanpher was mounting his horse, and a moment later rode away toward home. He was unsteady in his saddle and lost his hat, but did not stop to recover it.

It was probably ten minutes later that Smoky Cole rode out of the livery-stable and headed toward home. He was savagely drunk and took out his spite on his horse, which almost threw him off in front of the sheriff's office.

"Well, they're gone and I hope they never came back," declared the sheriff fervently.

"You and me both," agreed Lonesome wearily. "It's gittin so a fuf-feller can't even sleep around here. Next time I'll take a hammer and nails with me and nail their pants to the floor. I'll betcha they'll stay put next time I have to git out of mum-my sleep to correct 'em."

"You think you're a little so-and-so, don'tcha?" queried the sheriff sarcastically.

"Not such a little bit either," retorted Lonesome. "I've got the stren'th to hold up the law, y'betcha."

* * * *

Hashknife and Sleepy were riding in from the other end of town, and the sheriff watched them ride up to the front of the office and dismount. He was not exactly sure whether he liked these two punchers or not. Still their smiles were friendly enough, but he was not sure that they were not laughing at him.

"Howdy," greeted Hashknife. "How's tricks?"

"Tricks are fine," yelled Lonesome. "I jist pup-played a dinger. Lemme tell yuh about it."

And with great gusto and much stuttering, Lonesome told them how he had treated the two drunken punchers.

"And Fat Fleager thought he'd lost his hearin', 'cause he couldn't hear 'em shoot-in'," concluded Lonesome. "Mamma mine, I never done nothin' half as good before."

"Didja think they'd do that, when yuh took the shells out of their guns?" asked Hashknife.

"I wasn't sure of nothin'," admitted Lonesome, "but it sure worked out swell."

"Now they'll pack a grudge agin' you," declared the sheriff.

"And I'll pack a riot-gun," said Lonesome laughing.

"Kind of a tough place yuh got here," said Hashknife, sitting down on the sidewalk and producing his papers and tobacco. "Cattle fade out and folks get shot. You kinda got yore hands full, ain't yuh, sheriff?"

The sheriff nodded slowly and shoved his hands deeply into his pockets.

"Yeah, I reckon things are kinda unsettled, Hartley."

"You fellers find a job yet?" Thus Lonesome, as if to change the subject.

"Not yet," grinned Hashknife. "Jobs is scarce."

"If I wanted a job punchin' cows, I'd sure pass up the Ghost Hills range," observed the sheriff. "There's lots of better ranges than this, where there's always a need for top-hands."

"Yeah, I reckon that's right," agreed Hashknife. "It ain't noways the best. The Circle Cross is the best outfit around here, ain't it?"

"Yeah, I reckon it is. They run more cattle than any other outfit around here—or did until—say, did yuh go over to the Flying M? Old man Shappee might have a job for one of yuh. It's about four miles east of here. And there's the 66 outfit about seven miles kinda south of here."

"We was just ridin' around today," explained Hashknife. "We ran across the Tomahawk ranch-house, but they ain't hirin' nobody."

"That's a cinch," said Lonesome, grinning widely. "They never did hire anybody. Old Cassidy and Jimmy Droop-drawers done all the work. Mebbe Ben Lanpher is doin' somethin' since old Cassidy git into jail, but I doubt it. He's so soaked with hooch that he's no good to anybody."

"Who is this here Ben Lanpher?" asked Hashknife.

"Millionaire kid," grunted the sheriff. "His father owns half of the Circle Cross. Lives in Frisco, I think. Sent the kid out here to learn the cattle business and he took a post-graduate course in whisky and six-guns. He was at the Circle Cross for quite a while, but he got stuck on Cassidy's daughter, pulled off a quarrel with Jim Trainor and hooked up with the Tomahawk. He says he's goin' to marry that breed girl, but I doubt it."

"So do I," agreed Sleepy, and added quickly. "He'd never stay sober long enough for that."

Hashknife chuckled to himself and tried to catch Sleepy's eye, but Sleepy was busy examining his fingernails and would not look up.

"It's a wonder that his father wouldn't make him come home," said Hashknife. "Somebody'll kill him if he don't pull the kink out of his neck."

"Well, sir, he's got a nice father, too," observed the sheriff. "I kinda like Lanpher. Not a damn bit like the kid. He was here about a year or so ago—him and his wife and daughter."

"And that daughter is a dinger," wheezed Lonesome. "Prettiest girl I ever seen. She sure was a promisin' lookin' filly, but Jim Trainor kinda close-herded her all the time. By golly, there was a lot of punchers that'd given their right eye to even dance with her. Her ma high-toned everybody, but papa was sort of a harmless hoptoad."

Lonesome laughed and shook his head sadly.

"Mamma looked right over my huh-head, when I tried to shake hands with her. I told her to set her sights lower if she wanted to connect with me and she got sore. Anyway, I got papa drunk and he confided that he had high ideas for daughter. I often wonder if be hit what he was aimin' at."

"And they ain't been here since, eh?" This from Sleepy.

"Nope. Their little son stayed, thasall. And I'll tell a man that this country didn't draw much when they got him."

"Lots of cattle shipped out of here?" asked Hashknife.

"Ain't been for a while." The sheriff shook his head. "Oh, there's a few bein' shipped now and then, but no big shipments. The 66 outfit shipped some horses the other day, didn't they, Lonesome?"

"Gosh, I dunno," Lonesome yawned widely. "I never keep track of them kinda things. It keeps me busy knockin' down drunken bad-men. Ho-o-o—hum-m-m!"

"Why don'tcha try sleepin' for it?" asked Hashknife.

"Try it?" snorted the sheriff. "My God, he don't do nothin' else but sleep."

"Don't I?"

Lonesome slapped himself on the chest.

"I went out and cleaned up on the bad-men, while the sheriff planted himself over there on the sidewalk and got cockeyed from tryin' to watch both ways at once."

"Yuh should 'a' seen him, gents. He seen Smoky comin' one way and Bennie the other. Then he yelps:

"'Don'tcha start nothin'!' Ha, ha, ha, ha!"

Lonesome roared his mirth and the sheriff whirled and went into the office, quivering with indignation.

"Now he's mad at me," wailed Lonesome, "and I suppose he'll fire me, and I won't have no more job than a jackrabbit. That's just my luck."

"You think yore kinda smart, don'tcha?" growled the harassed sheriff.

"Well," Lonesome sighed gleefully, "it isn't as bad as I thought it was. When Fat gets to blamin' me for bein' smart, I know everythin' is all right."

Lonesome began manufacturing a cigaret and the conversation stopped for a few minutes. A loaded wagon creaked down the street, stirring up a cloud of dust. Over in front of the Antelope saloon a couple of cowpunchers mounted and rode away, arguing loudly over something that neither of them knew anything about. Up the street a couple of dogs started a battle, which was a signal to every dog in town to come and look on.

Hashknife inhaled deeply on his cigaret and motioned with his arm to take in the whole town.

"Boys, this is the kind of a town to live in. They can all have their cities—give me the old cow-town."

"Huh!"

Lonesome flipped away his match and stared at Hashknife.

"Pardner, you've got a hell of an idea of a place to live. You ain't been around much, have yuh?"

"No-o-o, not a whole lot."

"I guess you ain't."

"Here comes an old-timer," observed Sleepy, pointing up the street. "Betcha he struck the mother-lode."

It was a bearded old prospector, astride a bony, gray horse, and trailing him was a decrepit-looking pack-horse, with pack askew and a limp in one leg.

The one-man caravan came straight to the office and the bearded man shaded his eyes from the sun, as he spelled out the sheriff's sign over the door.

"Howdy, stranger," said Lonesome. "Somethin' I can do for yuh?"

"You the sheriff?" asked the bearded one anxiously.

"No, I'm his hired bad-man buster," grinned Lonesome.

Just then the sheriff came to the door, and Lonesome jerked his thumb in that direction.

"There's the sheriff—such as be is."

"What do yuh want?" queried the sheriff.

"Well—" The patriarch cleared his throat raspingly and leaned forward in his saddle— "I found a dead man a little while ago."

The Sheriff stepped out nearer him.

"Keep on talking stranger. Where'd yuh find him?"

"Back up the road a piece. Mebbe it's a couple of miles. He's layin' on his face in the middle of the road. I didn't move him none, I didn't, but I looked at him enough to know that he's dead. Been shot in the back of the head, 'cordin' to what I observed."

"What did he look like?" queried Lonesome.

"I told yuh he's layin' on his face—kinda rootin' into the dust. Got on chaps and overalls and a shirt. Jist a little ways before I finds this here dead man, I finds this in the road."

He drew a six-shooter from the waistband of his overalls and handed it to the sheriff. It was a Colt single-action .44 caliber.

"Say yuh found it in the road?" asked the sheriff, examining the gun closely.

"Yeah. I thinks to myself that I've found me a good gun, but when I finds the dead man, I decides to turn the gun over to the sheriff. It's been shot once."

"I see it has," nodded the sheriff, and then to Lonesome—

"Get a hack from the livery-stable and we'll go out after this dead man."

Lonesome bow-legged his way across the street and down to the stable, while the sheriff went back through his office to the stable, where he and Lonesome kept their saddle-horses.

The old prospector turned and studied the saloon signs across the street, spat dryly and rode over to the Antelope to quench a thirst that was probably of long standing.

"Who do yuh reckon got killed, Hashknife?" asked Sleepy, as they waited for the sheriff.

"Probably that fool Lanpher. Here comes the sheriff."

They swung on to their horses and joined Fleager, without waiting for Lonesome.

"He'll come along after while," assured the sheriff. "We'll go ahead and investigate."

It took them only a short time to reach the spot, where the man was lying. On both sides of the road was a heavy thicket of brush and rocks. The sheriff dismounted and turned the man over.

It was Smoky Cole. Hashknife and Sleepy swung down and the three of them made a minute examination. Cole had been shot from behind, the bullet striking him almost at the base of the brain.

"Never knowed what hit him," declared the sheriff, standing up and dusting his knees.

"His gun is still in its holster, too," said Hashknife as he drew the gun out and looked it over. All the chambers were loaded and the barrel was clean.

"Kinda looks like he never had a chance, sheriff."

The sheriff nodded gloomily and began searching for tracks in the deep dust.

"I wonder where Sandy Claws found that six-gun."

"Said it was a little beyond here," said Sleepy. "It was prob'ly beyond that curve, and we can likely see where he picked it up."

They left the body and walked up the road, searching for the place where the old man had dismounted to pick up the gun. About fifty yards beyond the first turn in the road they found the spot.

"Here's where the gun was dropped," observed the sheriff, pointing at the footprints in the road.

Hashknife was looking a little farther on, and now he crossed the road, reached into the brush and picked up a black sombrero.

"Here's a hat," he called, and walked back to the sheriff.

It was a fairly new Stetson, but badly soiled, and in the sweat-band was punched the initials "B. L."

"Ben Lanpher," declared the sheriff thoughtfully. "That's his hat. He probably bushwhacked Smoky and lost his hat and gun in his getaway. And he was likely so drunk that he never thought to stop and get 'em."

As they walked back to the body, Lonesome drove into view and managed to turn his team around near the body.

It did not take Lonesome long to find out all they knew and he shook his head sadly.

"I knowed it," he declared. "Yuh can't mix whisky and six-guns. Well," optimistically, "the county ain't loser none to speak about, Fat."

"Mebbe not," grunted the sheriff, and motioned for them to help him put the body into the hack.

Lonesome climbed back to his seat and the sheriff gave his orders where to deliver the body.

"Ain't you goin' back with us?" queried Lonesome.

"Nope, not now. I've got to go and get Ben Lanpher."

"Goin' to give him a medal?" grinned Lonesome.

"Goin' to arrest him for murder."

"Aw, for gosh sake! You don't call this murder, do yuh?"

"Well—" The sheriff mounted and adjusted his holster—"well, yuh couldn't very well call it self-defense, Lonesome. Smoky never drawed his gun, and he was shot from behind. No, I reckon Bennie is sure up ag'in' it good and strong."

The sheriff rode on toward the Tomabawk, while Lonesome spluttered at the team and drove back toward Wolf Wells, with Hashknife and Sleepy riding behind the wagon.

"Gosh, this sure will be a jolt to old man Lanpher," observed Sleepy sadly.

"Yeah," sighed Hashknife. "I sure feel sorry for them folks. I wonder if the sheriff knows Lanpher's address in Frisco."

"You know it, don't yuh?"

"Yeah, but I don't want anybody to know that I do."

He called to Lonesome and asked him about the Lanpher family.

"I don't know his address, and I don't reckon that Fat does either," replied Lonesome. "Jim Trainor'd know it."

"Suppose we ride to the Circle Cross and tell Trainor? He'd probably want to know about Smoky Cole."

"That's a good idea," admitted Lonesome. "You go ahead."

Lonesome drove on, and the two cowboys turned and rode back up the highway toward the Circle Cross.

Hashknife was very thoughtful, but finally turned to Sleepy.

"Cowboy, it kinda looks like we've bit off a big chaw."

"Sure does," agreed Sleepy, "and there don't seem to be no handy place to start chawin', does there?"

Hashknife shook his head, his eyes squinted thoughtfully.

"No, there don't, Sleepy. I reckon its a fact that a gang of rustlers are makin' a cleanup in this range, but everybody is scared to talk about it.

"It must 'a' been that gang who killed the two cattle detectives, but I don't think they had anythin' to do with this killin' today."

"Mebbe old man Cassidy is one of the gang," suggested Sleepy.

"Might be. As far as that's concerned, Ben Lanpher might be one of 'em, too. It looks to me like Smoky Cole tried to convict old Cassidy at that trial. He sure stuck for conviction. I'm just wonderin' if Smoky Cole didn't try to make love to Lorna Cassidy, and that was why the old man drew a dead-line against the Circle Cross outfit.

"Smoky was a mean sort of a jasper, and that would be his idea of revenge, to hang the old man. Still I don't think that Ben belongs to the rustlers, because he wouldn't hardly steal from his own father."

"How about that warning that Lorna told us about, Hashknife?"

"Don't mean anythin', Sleepy. They'd naturally want everybody to think they was sufferin', too. But where in hell are they disposin' of the stock? Workin' in the dark thisaway is kinda hard, don'tcha know it? And we can't ask a lot of fool questions, because we don't know when we're talkin' to some of the gang."

They passed the spot where Cole had been killed, and took the right-hand road at the forks, which wound in and out of the brushy coulées and into a wide swale on the bank of a creek where the Circle Cross buildings were located.

CHAPTER V

IT WAS growing late, but there was still enough light to show that the Circle Cross was no small outfit. The ranch-house was pretentious in size, the barns, fences and corrals were in good repair, and even the front yard of the ranch-house seemed well-kept.

"Looks like the teepee of a millionaire," observed Sleepy, as they dismounted at the ranch-house.

A fat Chinese answered their knock at the front door and nodded solemnly when they asked for Trainor.

"Yessah, he in. I call."

"Who's out there?" yelled Trainor's voice.

"This is Hartley," called Hashknife.

"Come on in and rest your feet."

They followed the Chinaman into the living-room, and in a few moments Trainor came in. He was carrying a bottle of liquor and some glasses, and seemed a trifle unsteady in his walk.

"Glad to see yuh," he boomed. "Welcome to the Circle Cross, gents. I've just been tryin' out some new liquor and I find that it has a lot of authority."

He started to pour out a glass.

"Say when, Hartley."

"When!" grunted Hashknife quickly.

"Say, that ain't half-full, cowboy. Why—"

"Too late in the afternoon, and we ain't been fed since breakfast."

"You ain't?" Trainor turned and yelled toward the kitchen.

"Hey, Quong! Throw on a couple of steaks. Cut 'em thick, yuh hear me?"

"Yessah, can do," called the Chinaman.

"Wait a minute," begged Hashknife. "We didn't come out here to bum a meal and a drink, Trainor; we came to tell you that Smoky Cole was killed a little while ago, and that the sheriff has gone to arrest Ben Lanpher for murder."

Trainor stared at Hashknife, started to put the bottle on the table, but missed, and it fell to the floor, where its contents gurgled out over a fine Navajo mg.

"Smoky Cole? How did this happen, Hartley?"

Hashknife explained how Cole's body had been found and how the evidence all pointed to Ben Lanpher. He told Trainor of the blood-less gun-fight at Wolf Wells, and that Ben Lanpher had ridden away ahead of Smoky Cole.

"And he shot Smoky from the brush, eh?" Trainor's jaw muscles bulged angrily. "Never gave him a chance. Wait a minute."

Trainor stepped out onto the front porch and yelled at two cow-punchers, who were down near a corral. Hashknife and Sleepy fol-lowed him out and watched the two men come up to them. Hashknife and Sleepy had never seen these two, and Trainor introduced them as "Buck" Avery and "Poco" Saunders.

Avery was a square-faced, pig-eyed, medium-sized man, about thirty years of age, whose face was badly marked from smallpox.

Saunders was of medium height, but thin-faced and as dark as a Mexican. His eyes were sullen and the pupils seemed flecked with red. After a searching glance, which seemed to take in every inch of both Hashknife and Sleepy, Saunders kept his eyes on Trainor's face, while Trainor repeated what Hashknife had told him.

Buck Avery swore witheringly, but Saunders said nothing when they learned that Smoky Cole was dead.

"We'll all have a drink and then go to town," said Trainor. "C'mon."

But Poco Saunders did not accept the invitation. He turned and walked back toward the corral, without a word.

"He was Smoky's bunkie," said Trainor, which seemed sufficient explanation for refusing to drink.

"Poco don't drink much, anyway," added Buck, "but I feel like a drink would kinda take the edge off a shock like that. It ain't that it's any surprise t'me, though. Smoky always got mean when he was drinkin', but he thought he was such a devil of a gunman that he'd git past with anythin'."

"He was shot from behind," reminded Sleepy.

"Which'll make it go hard with Ben Lanpher," nodded Buck over his drink. "It's a fine start for a kid like him, and I feel a lot more sorry for his folks than I do for him. Yuh goin' to wire 'em, ain'tcha, Trainor?"

"Just as soon as I get to town, Buck. Let's go."

Poco Saunders had saddled his horse and was waiting for them. Hashknife studied Poco, while Trainor and Buck Avery were saddling, and decided that Poco was a very sinister-looking young man; and might well be marked with a danger signal.

Whereas Smoky Cole was a talkative gunman, prone to boast of his prowess and more or less audible threatening, Poco would probably shoot first and talk about it later, if at all.

Trainor and Avery rode out from the corral, joined them, and the five of them headed for Wolf Wells at a gallop. Hashknife showed them where Smoky's body had been discovered, and where Ben Lanpher's gun and hat had been picked up, but Poco showed no interest in this.

Trainor looked curiously at Poco, who went on without them.

"Hit him kinda hard, I reckon," he observed. "Him and Smoky were bunkies for a long time. Poco's a good puncher, but he ain't got much sense."

"Part Mexican?" asked Hashknife.

"He's got some Mexican blood in him, I reckon," replied Buck. "Used to talk it a little once in a while. That's where he got his nickname."

They rode into town and went straight to the sheriff's office, where they found several men talking with the sheriff. He had brought Ben Lanpher back with him and had locked him in a cell.

"He was still drunk," said the sheriff, "and he sure was a meek jasper. Didn't object to bein' locked up, except to tell me he never done it. Mebbe he was so drunk that he didn't know when he shot Cole. I dunno."

"Man never gets so drunk that he don't remember bushwhackin' and killin' a man," declared Hashknife.

"Dang right he don't," agreed Lonesome Hobbs. "That ain't no alibi," and added sadly, "I wish I'd let their guns alone t' day. One or both of 'em would 'a' got killed, but it would 'a' been legal. I s'pose I've got to spend most of my time feedin' and takin' care of prisoners now. Thank gosh, we've only got two cells. If we get any more prisoners we'll have to pasture 'em out some'ers."

A man came across the street and joined the group. He was a sallow-faced man, with tobacco-stained teeth and ink-stained fingers.

"I was just comin' down to send a telegram to Lanpher," said Trainor, addressing the newcomer. "You heard what happened, didn't yuh, Whitey?"

"Yeah, I heard about it. Looks kinda bad for the kid."

Trainor walked away with Whitey, going to the depot, and Hashknife and Sleepy put their horses into a corral. At the depot, Trainor sent a long message to William Lanpher, giving him the details of the trouble.

"There's a telegram here for yuh, Trainor," said the depot agent, as he checked off the words on Trainor's message.

"I was goin' to send it out to yuh, if somebody was goin' out your way. This'll cost yuh a dollar and sixty cents."

Trainor paid for the message and walked out. At the edge of the platform he tore open the envelope and read the message, a serious frown on his face. Then he grinned softly and went back up the street.

* * * *

When Ben Lanpher sobered up he failed to become the least bit repentant over what had happened to him. Trainor had consulted with George Mitchell, the lawyer from San Francisco, and had hired him to defend Ben, but Ben would have none of him.

Hashknife and Sleepy talked with the sheriff about Lanpher.

"He's loco," declared the sheriff. "Tells a tale that no jury would believe."

"What about?" queried Hashknife.

"Aw, he says he never bushwhacked Cole a-tall."

"I'd like to talk with him a while," observed Hashknife, "and see if he tells the same thing twice."

"Might be a good idea," agreed Lonesome Hobbs. "Me and Fat'll listen and see what it sounds like."

"Prob'ly won't talk to yuh. Mitchell comes down here to have a talk with him, but he cussed Mitchell plumb out of the jail. Mitchell told him that Trainor hired him to defend him, and it made Lanpher sore as hell. I'll see if Ben'll talk to yuh."

The sheriff came back in a few minutes with the information that Ben was willing to talk to anybody who wasn't connected with the

Circle Cross outfit. They went through the office and into the rear, where two cells were built in at the back of the room.

Old Pinto Cassidy scowled at them through the bars, but noticed that they were strangers and became more friendly. Ben came to the barred door and squinted at Hashknife.

"I know you," he said hoarsely. "You're the jasper that winked over my shoulder. By God, that seems a long time ago. What did yuh want to see me for?"

"Ye don't have to talk with 'em, if ye don't want to, remimber that, Ben," warned Cassidy. "Ye have to be careful who ye talk wid in here. Sure, it's a hell of a place to be in, so it is."

"That's all right, Cassidy," grunted Ben. "I've nothin' to conceal."

"Then tell us about it," urged Hashknife. "What did you do after you left town yesterday?"

Ben forced a laugh and tried to peer around the corner of his door.

"I remember that Lonesome Hobbs played a dirty trick on me. After that I got on my horse and started home. I was pretty drunk—too drunk to ride fast, and I had a bad horse.

"I loaded my gun on the way, I remember that because I dropped some shells and got off to pick 'em up. I had a hard time getting back on my bronc, but finally made it.

"Then I seen Smoky Cole coming. He was quite a ways behind me, but he was foggin' right along as though he was tryin' to catch me. I didn't want him to catch me, because I was just sober enough to know that a killing out there might look like murder.

"I rode on, but had a lot of trouble with that damn horse of mine. He almost threw me a couple of times, and I guess we wasted a lot of time along that brushy road. All to once, I thought that Smoky was shootin' at me."

Ben grinned wearily and shook his head.

"No, I didn't see Smoky at all, but I sure heard him shoot. I drew my gun and waited for him to swing around the curve, but I guess I was just drunk enough to cause me to accidently pull the trigger. Anyway, I felt the gun kick out of my hand, and then that fool bronc started to buck again. That was the first time I ever shot off that horse, and I guess it was scared stiff.

"Anyway, we must have gone real fast, because I remember we were close to the Tomahawk when I got my reins back again. And that's all, except that the sheriff woke me up later on and told me I had killed Smoky Cole."

Hashknife nodded over his cigaret.

"That's the whole story," sighed Ben.

"And, by golly, it's a good one, too," added Cassidy. "You stick to that story, me lad. I stuck to mine—and look where I am."

Hashknife laughed at Cassidy. Squaw-man he might be; a bitter old cattleman he surely was, but he still retained his sense of humor.

"If Cole had been killed several days ago, you might be a free man now, Cassidy," said Hashknife.

"Ah, that's true, me lad; but I'd suffer a long time in jail, if the poor misguided lad could be brought back to life. He was but goin' accordin' to his own lights, so he was."

"Then he had a damn poor light!" snapped Ben.

"A lot of us have," sighed Cassidy. "Mine has flickered badly at times. 'Tis hard to sit here the long days and know that me old ranch has no keeper, except Lorna and Jimmy. Sure, that's no job for a bit of a lass and a well-meanin', but poor managin' lad. They'll hold me and Bennie for the nixt term of court, which will be a long, long time away."

"Don't worry about that," assured Sleepy. "We'll do what we can to help yuh out."

"Well, now that's nice of ye," said Cassidy, scratching his head as if wondering why these strangers would promise to help him in any way.

"What do you think of my story?" asked Ben anxiously.

"I dunno," Hashknife shook his head. "It sounds reasonable, Lanpher—to me. But they'll likely hold you for the next term of court. You've got an even break thasall."

"That's all I want."

As they started away, Cassidy called to them:

"Come again, lads. Ye'r the first folks I ever known in Wolf Wells that showed common sense. Ye'll probably not find us out when ye come again."

"All right," laughed Hashknife as they passed out and shut the door behind them.

The sheriff and Lonesome had heard every word, and nodded to the two cow-punchers.

"Same story," said Lonesome, leading the way outside. "Ben sure has got it rehearsed well, or he's tellin' the truth."

"Sounds reasonable, at that," commented Hashknife. "He shot the gun accidental, got his hat bucked off. But who in thunder killed Smoky Cole, if Ben Lanpher didn't?"

The sheriff scowled and shook his head.

"I dunno of anybody that would bushwhack him, Hartley."

"It's kinda gettin' to be a habit around here, ain't it? Trainer has lost two other men in the same way."

"Yeah," breathed the sheriff, "damn it! It makes me nervous to think about it. Feller never knows who's next."

The sheriff looked so lugubrious that Hashknife laughed and slapped him on the shoulder.

"I reckon yo're safe, as long as yuh don't antagonize the bush-whackers," said Hashknife.

"Huh! Well, I dunno."

Poco Saunders came into the upper end of town, dismounted at the Lily of the Valley hitch-rack, and walked down to them. Poco had a queer, stiff-legged walk, and held his elbows dose to his sides.

"Trainor said he wanted to see yuh," he told Hashknife.

"What's he got on his mind?" queried Hashknife.

"I dunno. Bronc stepped on his foot this mornin', and he can't walk. Mebbe he wants to hire yuh? I dunno."

"Did he ask for both of us?" queried Sleepy.

Poco shook his head, turned on his heel and went back toward the saloon.

"He's a queer jigger," observed Lonesome; "dangdest feller to run out of words thataway."

"He don't talk much, that's a cinch," grinned Hashknife, getting to his feet. "I reckon we'll get a bit to eat, Sleepy."

They walked up to a restaurant and ordered a meal. It was not like Hashknife to accept a job alone, but the circumstances were, different this time.

"Well, whatcha goin' to do about it?" asked Sleepy.

"I been wonderin' a lot m'self, Sleepy. Suppose you go out to the Tomahawk and help 'em out a little, cowboy. Keep yore eyes open and yore mouth shut; sabe? I'll take this Circle Cross job, if that's what Trainor wants.

"But—" Hashknife put his hand on Sleepy's arm and spoke softly—"for gosh sake, look out. I've got a feelin' that we're marked right now. This is goin' to be our hardest job, Sleepy. Yuh can't dodge a bullet that's fired at yore back—and that's their game. There's a dirty bunch of murderers in these hills, and they'll hand us a harp if they get a chance."

"But there ain't' nothin' to work on," complained Sleepy. "They won't come out into the open and everybody's afraid to say what they think. I'll find out what I ran without askin' questions, and if I do stumble on to anythin' worth talkin' about, I'll see yuh real quick."

They finished their meal and went to the corral after their horses. Poco Saunders saw them ride past the saloon, but made no move to join them. About half-way to where the road forked to the Circle Cross, they met Jimmy, the half-breed, from the Tomahawk.

He grinned widely and drew up his broncho.

"You go Tomahawk?" he asked.

"I'm goin' out there," said Sleepy. "Maybe I stay and help for a while."

"That damn good! Both go?"

"No," Hashknife shook his head. "I'm goin' to work for the Circle Cross, Jimmy."

"Not good," Jimmy shook his head.

"You don't like the Circle Cross?"

"No, by God!"

And then to Sleepy—

"I be back soon."

He spurred his horse ahead and faded out in a cloud of dust.

"The Tomahawk sure does love the Circle Cross," laughed Hashknife. "No wonder they drew a dead-line. Find out what it was all about, Sleepy. Prob'ly just a personal affair, but we've got to consider everything around here. But don't come bustin' over with the first thing yuh find out. Let it soak into yore mind, cowboy."

They shook hands at the forks of the road and went on their different ways. They had fought their range-battles together for so long that they both felt a trifle helpless apart.

"Some day they'll get us both," mused Hashknife, as he rode slowly along the dusty road. "Yuh can dodge bullets just so long, but they'll get yuh in the end. Dang Sleepy! If he'll only keep his darned eyes open. He needs a keeper, that's what he needs. Mebbe I won't like this Circle Cross job—mebbe."

He found Jim Trainor sitting in an easy chair on the ranch-house porch, a bottle beside him and his right foot swathed in bandages.

"Put up your bronc, Hartley," he called. "You've got a job. Buck will show yuh where to put him."

Buck Avery called from the bunk-house and joined Hashknife at the barn, where they stabled the horse.

"Bronc stepped on Jim's foot," explained Buck. "Dang fool won't send for a doctor, so he can suffer for all of me. Yuh seen Poco, did yuh?"

"Yeah, he sent me out."

They sauntered up to the ranch-house and Trainor yelled for Quong to bring two more glasses. Trainor was already half-drunk, but in a good humor.

"I was wonderin' if Poco would find yuh before yuh got another job," he explained. "You're a top-hand, I can see that, Hartley. Losin' Smoky Cole kinda puts me short-handed, and now I go and get walked on. Damn horse was sharp-shod, too. Pour your own drinks, gents.

"I ought to be gettin' an answer from Lanpher pretty soon. I found Mitchell, that lawyer, and told him to take the kid's case, but the kid cussed the hell out of him. That sure is appreciation. I suppose things will have to ride about like they are until Lanpher shows up from Frisco and looks things over. What do you think of the case, Hartley?"

"Well, it kinda looks like the kid was guilty," observed Hashknife. "Mebbe the law will consider that they were both drunk at the time; but that's a poor defense. A feller ain't so awful drunk when he'll bushwhack a man and kill him the first shot."

"Ben Lanpher is a good shot, too," said Buck Avery. "He never did do nothin' but drink whisky and practise shootin'."

"Two bad things to mix," declared Trainor thoughtfully, and then—

"Where's your partner, Hartley?"

Hashknife looked up quickly.

"Did yuh want to hire him, too?"

"Want to—yes; but I haven't work enough."

"He went out to the Tomahawk ranch. Sleepy's always doin' somethin' for folks, and he kinda thought mebbe they'd need a little help. This deal makes it kinda tough for the Tomahawk."

"That's a fact," Trainor scowled at his glass, shaking his head sadly. "Yuh know, I should 'a' sent one of the boys over there to help 'em out."

"They'd be welcome," laughed Buck. "Welcome, like the small-pox."

"Me and Sleepy came past there a while back," volunteered Hashknife. "Wasn't sure just what ranch it was, but we was kinda dry; so we stopped for a drink. They treated us fine."

"You were lucky," said Trainor, pouring himself another drink. "You work for me and you won't dare go over there."

"They didn't look dangerous. Nobody there, except the old lady, the girl and the half-breed puncher."

"Uh-huh," Trainor's voice was mildly sarcastic. "Don't under-rate that half-breed, Hartley. He's one of the best rifle-shots you ever seen."

"Yeah?" Hashknife leaned back against a porch-post and hugged his knees.

"Yuh know, I've never seen such a country for crack-shots as this is. Mostly everybody I've heard spoken about has that reputation. If trouble ever starts there won't be more'n one box of shells needed to kill off the whole danged population." Trainor laughed boisterously and handed the bottle to Buck.

"We sure can shoot, can't we, Buck? I betcha Hartley can shoot a few, too, eh, Hartley?"

Hashknife shook his head.

"No-o-o, I wouldn't say that, Trainor. Me and Sleepy never put ourselves up to be good shots, but we're willin' shooters. Lotsa folks can out-shoot us, but," Hashknife grinned softly, "we're still alive."

"And some of them ain't, eh?" grinned Buck suggestively.

"Every dog has its day," said Hashknife slowly. "None of us can live forever. I always forked on the theory that bein' right gives yuh the edge on folks that do wrong. That's why a horse-thief goes to the end of his rope in a short time. A gunman cuts a short swath. If yuh notice, they don't last long, and it's because they're all wrong. Look at Smoky Cole. Look at Ben Lanpher."

"Your theory don't work out right, Hartley," laughed Trainor. "It wasn't a case of right winnin' out there. Ben Lanpher wasn't any more right than Smoky."

"All right—where's Ben Lanpher? The law got him, and the law is right."

"Oh, to hell with such arguments!" blurted Trainor. "Fill up your glass, Hartley. Here comes Poco. Didja tell him to get the mail, Buck?"

"Yeah, I told him," said Buck.

Poco rode down to the stable, put up his horse and came slowly up to the house. He nodded to Hashknife and handed Trainor a telegram. Buck offered Poco a glass and the bottle, but the flinty-faced cowpuncher refused with a shrug of his thin shoulders.

"Telegram from William Lanpher," explained Trainor. "He'll arrive at Wolf Wells tomorrow night. Don't say whether he's alone or not. damn it, I told him he ought to take Ben home months ago, but he wouldn't do it."

"Ben is of age," grunted Buck. "He had a birthday about a month ago and celebrated it by gettin' drunk and shootin' at himself in the Antelope mirror. There was busted glass all over the place. Somebody said he'd have bad luck for seven years."

"Mrs. Lanpher'll probably come," said Trainor thickly. "She thinks Ben's a little tin god."

"He's her son." Thus Poco Saunders, speaking for the first time since he arrived.

"He ain't worth worryin' about, that's a cinch," laughed Trainor.

"Good or bad, their mother worries," said Poco flatly, and got to his feet.

He started to say something more, but changed his mind and went down to the bunk-house.

Hashknife looked after him and squinted thoughtfully. He had disliked Poco Saunders—until that remark. It showed that somewhere inside that minister-looking cow-puncher was a big spark of human nature.

"Good or bad, their mother worries," repeated Hashknife to himself. "She thinks that Ben is a tin-god—but he's her son."

"Queer sort of a jigger," said Buck, noticing that Hashknife was looking toward the bunk-house.

"Poco don't drink like other folks. He won't take a drink until he is ready to get drunk. Then he hides his gun, and proceeds to get goshawful drunk. He won't talk much, but he's no fool, Poco ain't."

"No, I betcha he ain't," agreed Hashknife. "If I was goin' to pick an enemy, I sure wouldn't pick Poco Saunders."

"The killin' of Smoky Cole kinda hit him hard," said Buck. "He used to grin once in a while, but now he goes around with the same hard-faced expression all the time. I'll bet he'd make a scrap-heap out of Ben Lanpher, if he had the chance."

"Aw, to hell with 'em all!" snorted Trainor. "Hey! Quong! Bring us another bottle. I'm celebratin' a busted foot and I need a lot of liquor."

"Ex-cuse me then," laughed Hashknife apologetically, "my stummick ain't in good shape, and I never did need much liquor. I'll go down and get used to the bunk-house."

Trainor frowned slightly, but gave a drunken shrug of his shoulders.

"You know your own insides, Hartley. If me and Buck get plumb paralyzed, you and Poco run the ranch, will yuh?"

"We'll do our best," laughed Hashknife, and went down to the bunk-house, where he found Poco Saunders playing solitaire.

Poco nodded, but kept on with his game.

"Which bunk do I take?" asked Hashknife.

Poco pointed out two unoccupied bunks and began rolling a cigaret. His tobacco sack was almost empty, so Hashknife tossed a full sack in front of him. He nodded his thanks and finished his cigaret. Suddenly he turned and looked straight at Hashknife.

"Do you think that Ben Lanpher killed Smoky Cole?"

Hashknife's face did not change a line, but his eyes squinted a trifle, as he replied—

"What makes yuh think he didn't, Saunders?"

Poco turned back to the table and gathered up the cards.

"I was just wonderin'," he said slowly. "Lanpher was pretty drunk."

"If Ben didn't kill him, who did?" asked Hashknife.

He had asked the same question several times, but no one had given him the slightest clue to show who might have done the murder. And he was doomed to disappointment this time. Poco inhaled deeply and shuffled the cards.

"There was several of that jury that was sore at him," reminded Hashknife.

"Not sore enough to murder him."

"Lotsa folks seem to think that Smoky Cole got what was comin' to him."

"Thasso?" Poco scowled thoughtfully at his cards, and tinned slowly, facing Hashknife.

"They say that Smoky wasn't any good, Hartley. He drank and raised hell in general every time he got money enough. Smoky was a gunman, and mebbe, accordin' to law, he wasn't just the sweetest little citizen yuh' could imagine; but he was my bunkie.

"Me and Smoky shared the same blanket for a long time. We split fifty-fifty on everythin'—me and Smoky did. He might 'a' been an enemy of society, as the judge said at Cassidy's trial, speakin' about criminals, but he was a good friend of mine."

Poco shifted his eyes and looked out through the dusty window, where the last rays of the sunset back-lighted the old cottonwoods beyond the creek, and the lines of his face softened until he was no longer the sinister-looking cowboy.

"He was my bunkie—my pal," he said softly.

"I reckon I understand," said Hashknife slowly. "I've got a bunkie, too, Saunders."

Poco turned and looked at him, as he got slowly to his feet and walked over to the door.

"I know yuh have," said Poco softly, "and—and yuh might tell him to look out."

Hashknife squinted wonderingly, as Poco shut the door behind him.

"What does he know?" wondered Hashknife, half-aloud. "And why does he tell me to warn Sleepy?"

There was no question that Poco Saunders knew something; that he did not believe Ben Lanpher guilty of murder. Hashknife wondered if Poco knew something about the Fantom Riders, who were making inroads on the cattlemen of the Ghost Hills Range; and was afraid to name them.

"It's too foggy for me to see through," he decided, "so I reckon we'll have to let nature take her course."

Came the musical clanging of the cook's triangle, which announced that supper was ready at the Circle Cross. As Hashknife stepped outside, Poco Saunders was crossing from the barn.

"We'll feed alone t'night," he observed, motioning toward the front porch of the ranch-house.

"Trainor and Buck ate both paralyzed drunk."

"Do they make a practise of drinkin' each other to sleep?" asked Hashknife.

"No. Trainor don't drink much, and Buck only cuts loose once a month. Help yourself to a wash-pan."

CHAPTER VI

THE next day, neither Trainor nor Buck Avery was in any shape for active duties. Hashknife asked Trainor what he wanted done, and Trainor was so muddled in the head that he had no coherent ideas. He finally told Hashknife to do what he pleased; so Hashknife saddled his gray bronco and headed into the hills, cutting across toward the Tomahawk.

He wanted to find Sleepy and tell him what Poco Saunders had said; but most of all he wanted to see if Sleepy was all right.

Circle Cross, Tomahawk and Flying M cattle dotted the hills, but the Circle Cross predominated. The feed was fairly good and there seemed plenty of water. It was an ideal range as far as nature was concerned.

As he swung higher into the hills he could see the town of Wolf Wells, a blur of buildings in the swale-like little valley, and beyond that drifted the smoke of a train. There was little color in the hills. Even the foliage of the few trees was of a gray tint that blended into the gray of the forbidding-looking hills.

"Ghost Hills is the right name for 'em," he told his horse, as he swung along a hogback, which led to the little valley of the Tomahawk ranch.

He found Sleepy humped up in the doorway of the ranch-house, trying to coax a tune out of a one-string mandolin, while Lorna leaned against the wall and smiled at his serious efforts.

"Hyah, cowboy!" yelled Sleepy. "By gosh, I'm glad for to see yuh. Git down and listen to the 'Cowboy's Lament,' done to a turn on one string."

Hashknife dismounted and came up to the doorway. Lorna nodded to him, but it was plainly evident that he was not exactly welcome, and he blamed it to the fact that he was working for the Circle Cross. Mrs. Cassidy came to the door, bobbed her head and went back to her work.

"Here, you play it, Lorna," Sleepy handed her the mandolin, and grinned at Hashknife. "She can play it, too."

But Lorna did not seem disposed to exhibit her musical ability. She took the instrument and went into the house.

"Callin' her by her first name already, eh?" chided Hashknife seriously.

Sleepy blushed and rubbed his stubbled chin.

"Well, there ain't no harm in that, is there?"

"No-o-o, I s'pose not. Lemme tell yuh somethin', cowboy."

And in a few words, Hashknife repeated what Poco Saunders had said.

"What do yuh reckon he meant?" asked Sleepy. "Look out for what?"

"Just that, and no more, Sleepy. I tell yuh, they're on to us and Poco knows it."

"Yeah, and Poco's probably one of the gang."

"If he is, why should he warn us?"

Sleepy shook his head violently.

"That's what I hate about this damn country, Hashknife. They're all too scared to talk. But I found out that the Tomahawk has lost a lot of stock. And old Cassidy never killed that detective, no more than I did. There's a bad, bad gang back in these hills, cowboy; and they swoop out and strike hard at anybody that horns into their business."

"Want to pick up and drift out?" queried Hashknife.

Sleepy glanced back at the doorway and shook his head.

"No more than you do, Hashknife. We'll strike a lead pretty soon. I tried to pump the half-breed puncher, but he's closemouthed like all Injuns. Mebbe he don't know any more than we do, but he's scared to talk."

"Suppose we take a ride into the hills," suggested Hashknife. "We'll kinda look around and see what we can see."

"That's a pious idea," agreed Sleepy, "I'll get my horse."

Lorna stood in the doorway and watched them ride away. Sleepy waved at her, but she made no move to show that she had seen him.

"Yo're free, white and twenty-one," said Hashknife, "but you ain't above takin friendly advice, are yuh, Sleepy?"

"Well, I ain't makin' love to her—if that's what yuh mean."

"Yuh don't have to make love, cowboy. It's already made. Do yuh know what I mean?"

"Yore advice is accepted," grinned Sleepy. "Let's forget the female end of this proposition."

They rode straight back to the main divide of the Ghost Hills, and swung in a wide circle. It was a wild range, where an army might be able to hide without fear of detection. They found two deserted old cabins, windowless and doorless, where the range horses sought shelter from the flies; but there were no other signs of human habitation.

It was nearly sundown when they came back to the Tomahawk. Jimmy, the half-breed, was there and greeted them with a grin. Hashknife did not dismount, but rode back to the Circle Cross, where he found supper on the table, Buck half-drunk again and Trainor swearing at his sore foot. Poco was eating supper.

Buck was just drunk enough to be quarrelsome, and insisted that he was going down to meet the Lanpher family, or as many of them as were coming that night.

Trainor was just as emphatic in telling Buck that he was seven kinds of a fool to even think he was. Trainor appealed to Hashknife.

"He'd be a fine lookin' thing to meet the owner of this ranch, wouldn't he? Wouldn't Mrs. Lanpher and Helen appreciate havin' him meet 'em, Hartley?"

"Well," grinned Hashknife, "I dunno them folks, but I reckon yo're right."

Buck exploded with protestations that he was as sober as a judge, and called upon Poco to look upon him and see if he—Buck—wasn't fit to meet a king and queen.

But Poco refused to be drawn into the argument and Buck subsided in a chair, where he began to snore.

"I don't like to ask it of yuh, Hartley," said Trainor, "but would yuh mind meetin' them folks and bringin' 'em out here? They'll be in about nine o'clock tonight, if the tram is on time, which it probably won't be.

"You can get a two-seated hack at the livery-stable and lead your horse back. Yuh won't be able to miss 'em, 'cause we don't have many strangers come into Wolf Wells."

"Sure, I'll go after 'em, Trainor. As soon as I get through eatin' a bit of supper, I'll go right down-town."

"Take yore time, Hartley. I'm goin' to bed right now. This danged foot is givin' me thunder tonight, and I drank too much last night. Feller's a fool to drink whisky." Hashknife sat down across from Poco and accepted of Quong's culinary art. He had not eaten since breakfast, and the fat Celestial grinned with delight as Hashknife stowed away great quantities of food.

"Belly good," observed Quong, "Cook plenty—nobody eat. Too much whisky, yo' sabe? Yo' eat good, I'm ve'y glad."

"Then I'll make yuh glad a lot of times," laughed Hashknife

* * * *

Hashknife took his time, and it was growing dark when he mounted his gray bronco and headed for Wolf Wells. Just before he reached the forks of the road he saw a rider pass, going toward town.

It was a little too far for identification, but he noted that the man was riding a gray or a grayish-roan horse. The rider had disappeared when Hashknife reached the main road, and he made no effort to overtake him.

The air was cool and Hashknife had plenty of time to go to town and arrange for the livery-rig before train-time. He was riding slowly, scanning the road, near the spot where Ben Lanpher's gun had been found, when the whip-like report of a rifle sounded from left.

Hashknife's horse swerved quickly, and for a moment Hashknife thought the shot had been fired at him, but there had been no sound from a bullet. He dropped off his horse, drew his six-shooter and led the horse down the road.

There were no more shots. The fringe of timber and brush along the road masked him from the hillside, but also precluded any chance of his seeing the shooter.

He led his horse around the first turn and stopped short. Almost at the same spot where Smoky Cole had been killed stood a man and a horse. The man appeared to be leaning against the horse, as if bracing himself, but when he saw Hashknife he threw up a six-shooter and fired.

Hashknife instinctively ducked, but the bullet hummed off through the brush ten feet away, and the man mounted swiftly although awkwardly and raced down the road.

Hashknife threw up his gun, but snapped it back into its holster, as he mounted swiftly and spurred after the rider.

He knew the speed of his gray horse, and felt sure that he could run his quarry down, if they kept to the road.

"Left handed son-of-a-gun!" snorted Hashknife. "Can't shoot straight, that's a cinch. C'mon, bronc!"

They whirled out into the more open country and Hashknife grinned to see that the rider was still traveling down the road. But the horse ahead, even with its long handicap start, was no match for the long-legged gray, which cut down its lead at every stride.

The rider looked wildly back and even turned in his saddle and tried to get into position for another shot, but, as the running gray horse drew closer, he jerked up on his reins and threw up his hands in token of surrender.

"Don't shoot!" he called, and Hashknife squinted through a cloud of dust at the face of Jimmy, the half-breed.

Hashknife moved in closer and noticed that Jimmy's right arm was bleeding badly.

"That's why yuh shot left-handed, eh?" panted Hashknife.

"Yeah," Jimmy nodded quickly. "Other arm no good."

"Who shot yuh?"

Jimmy squinted at Hashknife and licked his lips.

"You don't shoot me?" he asked.

"No. I heard the shot. Then you shot at me?"

Jimmy nodded and felt of his arm tenderly.

"I thought you shoot me, but I guess not. You can't be two place same time. Who shoot me, you s'pose?"

"Hard to tell, Jimmy. Is your arm hurt bad?"

"Pretty bad. Almost knock me off horse."

He rolled up his sleeve and they examined the wound. The bullet had struck near the wrist and had cut a furrow almost to the elbow. It was a painful, but not a serious wound; and Hashknife bound it up with a big handkerchief.

"How in thunder did yuh get hit in that arm?" queried Hashknife. "The shot came from the left-side of the road."

"I dunno," said Jimmy blankly. "I reach up to rub my nose, I think."

"By gosh, that was close!" exploded Hashknife, "that bullet must 'a' passed close to yore chin, hooked into yore wrist and kicked loose at your elbow. Now, who in hell wants to kill you, Jimmy?"

Jimmy's eyes were troubled as he thought deeply, but his answer was not at all evasive:

"I dunno. I never hurt nobody."

"All right, Jimmy; let's be driftin'."

"I go after coffee," explained Jimmy. "Lorna want coffee for Sleepy."

Hashknife grinned widely, as they rode on, but deep in his heart he was afraid that Sleepy might fall in love with this half-breed girl. But he forgot that as he studied Jimmy and his grayish-roan horse.

It would have been easy to mistake them in that light for himself and the gray horse, he reflected. Were the Fantom Riders aware that he and Sleepy were trying to smoke them out, and were trying to ambush them?

If that were the case, they would get them sooner or later. Hashknife shuddered slightly. He was convinced that they had mistaken their man and had injured Jimmy. There was no way to guard against an ambush. They would likely try another place next time. He turned to Jimmy.

"You better see a doctor about that arm, Jimmy. I'll pay the bill."

"No," Jimmy shook his head quickly. "I go back and let Minnie fix it. She know how."

"Minnie is Mrs. Cassidy, ain't she?"

"Yeah."

"Are you and Lorna related?"

"Hell no! My mother and Minnie sisters, thasall."

Hashknife grinned, but did not try to explain that Jimmy and Lorna were cousins. Anyway, it would mean nothing to Jimmy.

Hashknife left Jimmy at the general store and went to arrange for the livery-rig. He knew that Jimmy would not discuss the shooting with any one. Coming back from the livery-stable he found the sheriff at his office.

"Lanpher's comin', eh? said the sheriff, after Hashknife had spoken of meeting him at the depot.

"The rest of the family comin'?"

"I dunno. The telegram didn't say, but Trainor talks like they was all comin'."

"I kinda feel sorry for them folks," mused the sheriff. "I like Lanpher. Never did get acquainted with his wife and daughter. I reckon I'll go over with yuh and meet 'em."

Contrary to predictions the train was on time. Lanpher, his wife and daughter were all there, with innumerable bags and suitcases. Hashknife was lucky enough to reach Lanpher first, and gave him the whispered warning—

"Remember, you don't know me."

Then came the sheriff, hand outstretched.

"Glad to meetcha ag'in, Lanpher; but not under these circumstances."

Lanpher shook hands with him, and asked—

"Can we see Ben?"

"Sure thing, yuh can. He don't know yo're comin', but I'll bet he'll be glad to see yuh all. Hartley'll take case of yore things."

Hashknife was glad to get them out of his way, while he loaded the baggage. He drove the team down to the sheriff's office and waited for them to finish their visit. They were in there quite a while, and had nothing to say when they climbed into the two-seater and headed for the ranch.

Lanpher rode with Hashknife on the front seat, and after they were out of the town he asked—

"Well, what have you found out, Hartley?"

"We've found out that a man's life ain't worth a plugged dime, Lanpher. As far as the rustlers are concerned, they're as safe as ever. We can't find out a thing. I'm with the Circle Cross and Sleepy is with the Tomahawk; but we'll both be cowboy angels pretty soon, I reckon."

"But they do not know what you are doing here," protested Lanpher.

"Don't they? That's fine," Hashknife laughed softly. "There's been a leak somewhere, Lanpher. They sure do know us. You didn't wire anybody, did yuh?"

"No, I did not. I was willing to let you two run this to suit your-selves, Hartley. I wired Trainor that we were coming, but that is the only wire I have sent him since you were at my home."

"It's sure got me fightin' my head," admitted Hashknife.

"What do you make of the case against Ben?"

"Well, it looks to me like another Fantom Rider deal, and Ben accidently happens along and gets the blame for it. He didn't kill Smoky Cole."

"I want to thank you for that," said Mrs. Lanpher brokenly. "It is good to think that some one besides us believe him innocent."

"Cassidy is very bitter," said Lanpher, after a long pause. "He cursed me in the jail a while ago. He seemes to blame me for what has happened to him, but I had nothing to do with it. The sheriff told me that Trainor was crippled."

"Yeah, I forgot to tell yuh that. A horse stepped on him."

"Too bad. What do you think of the Circle Cross?"

"Dunno yet. Looks like a rich ranch."

"Rich! Say, you'd be surprized to know what that ranch has al-ready cost me, Hartley. I'd sell out in a minute, if I could get back what I've spent on it."

"I'll betcha. Hills are pretty tonight, ain't they?"

They drove up to the ranch-house and Trainor hobbled out to meet them, with the aid of a cane. Hashknife unloaded the baggage and placed it on the porch, while they went into the house.

Then he drove to the barn, unhitched the horses, stabled them and went to the bunk-house where he found Buck and Poco snor-ing a duet. Buck had a half-empty whisky-bottle on a chair beside his bunk, and one of his boots had been placed upside down over a bunk-post.

Hashknife rolled a cigaret and sat down on the edge of his bunk to remove his boots. Poco stirred, sat up, his eyes filled with sleep. He squinted at Hashknife, grunted a hoarse greeting and slumped back on to his pillow. One of Poco's hands was exposed and Hashknife noticed that there was a circle of whang-leather around his wrist. He looked closer, when he saw that a leather thong ran from the wrist under the blanket, and was drawn taut.

Poco's cartridge belt was hanging from the bunk-post, and over this was hung a coat, but when Hashknife crossed to the table to light his cigaret from over the chimney of the oil-lamp, he was able to see that the holster was empty.

Hashknife went back, undressed and blew out the lamp. He sat on the edge of the bunk for a long time, but finally crawled between the blankets and placed his six-shooter under the blanket beside him.

"Poco is scared of somethin'," mused Hashknife. "He's got his six-gun linked to him—and a feller don't anchor himself to a thing like that to keep from fallin' out of bed. Dang him, I'd like to trade talk with him. But I reckon he's scared like everybody else—and me included."

* * * *

"Buck is goin' over to the Flyin' M to see old man Shappee for me, and Poco is goin' to drive an extra team to town; so we can get rid of this livery-outfit. You can go with Buck, if yuh want to, or yuh can stay here and see what yuh can do about fixin' up the fence of the brandin' corral."

Trainor had hobbled down to the barn, with the aid of a cane, and was talking with Hashknife while Poco and Buck harnessed the teams.

"Well, yo're the boss," smiled Hashknife. "I'll go with Buck if yuh say so; but it don't take two men to pack a message. Mebbe I better fix up that fence."

"Whatever yuh want to do, Hartley. Mr. and Mrs. Lanpher want to go down and see Ben; so I'll go with 'em. Miss Lanpher has a bad headache and will stay home."

"All right, I'll stay here and help Quong run the ranch."

Poco drove away with the ranch-wagon, while Buck drove up to the house with the livery-rig, picked up the Lanphers and Trainor and drove away.

Hashknife secured a hammer and nails and worked on the corral for a time; but Hashknife was no carpenter and the work palled. Anyway, it was too hot to work. He went back and sat down in the shade of the bunk-house. Somehow, he felt much safer with a solid wall at his back.

Miss Lanpher came out on the ranch-house porch and sat down with a magazine. She glanced idly through it for a while, but put it aside and looked around.

Hashknife got up and walked to the porch.

"Mornin', Miss Lanpher. How's the headache?"

She looked at him closely, frowned slightly and said—

"I do not believe I have ever met you."

"Yes'm, yuh have," he smiled. "Me and Sleepy was at your house in Frisco not long ago. Yore pa introduced us."

"Perhaps," she nodded coldly, "but I do not remember you. Are you one of the cowboys?"

"Well," Hashknife scratched his head thoughtfully, "yuh might brand me as such. I brought yuh in from Wolf Wells last night, if yuh remember."

"Oh, you were the driver."

She picked up the magazine and opened it before she looked at him and said—

"Is there something I can do for you?"

Hashknife's smile faded and he studied her for a moment.

"Yes'm, I was just kinda wonderin', don'tcha know it?"

"Well?" Icily.

"Just kinda wonderin' if it's the fogs that make Frisco folks so chilly."

She looked questioningly at him, as if at a loss to know what he meant; but he merely turned, put on his hat and walked back toward the bunk-house.

"That was a damn mean thing to say," he chuckled to himself. "But she's prob'ly so high-toned that she'd have to have it explained to her."

He went back to the corral and spent the rest of the morning hammering lustily. The ringing of the triangle, as Quong announced the mid-day meal, caused him to hang up his hammer and admire the collection of bruises he had acquired.

Quong was standing just outside the kitchen, fanning himself with a towel as Hashknife came striding across the yard, heading for the wash-bench.

Suddenly he jolted hard in his stride and jerked sidewise. An angry bee had buzzed past his head, or what had seemed to be a whizzer of some sort; but the buzz was punctuated by a loud—

Whap!

Quong dropped his towel and jerked away, staring wildly at the door-casing behind him, where a bullet had drilled a neat hole.

"Zee-e-e-e—blam!"

Then came the thin, far-away crack of a rifle. Quong fairly fell into the kitchen, and Hashknife was right on his heels.

The second bullet had gone in through the doorway and had torn a gaping hole in Quong's big copper kettle on the stove, and the soup was spewing out all over the hot griddles.

The room was filled with steam and odors of burning grease, plentifully mixed with Celestial chatter that might be oaths or prayers.

Hashknife grasped a cloth and managed to fling the kettle outside. Miss Lanpher came to the door from the dining-room, wondering at the turmoil. She stared around, and Quong caught sight of her. He immediately began bombarding her with pidgin-English, but Hashknife stopped him.

"Wait a minute, Quong," and then to Miss Lanpher—

"Miss Lanpher, this is Quong, the cook. Quong, this is Miss Lanpher."

Hashknife stepped gracefully back and motioned for Quong to continue, but Quong had forgotten what to say, and turned back to his stove.

Miss Lanpher looked coldly at Hashknife and her eyebrows lifted a trifle, as she said:

"That was very thoughtful of you, I am sure. But I have known Quong a long time. I was here several weeks about a year ago."

"Oh, yeah. Well, it was my mistake, ma'am."

"Now, what happened in here, Mr. Hartley?"

"Well, Miss Lanpher; somebody took two shots at the cook and ventilated the soup-pot. Nothin' serious."

"Took a shot at the cook?" she gasped. "Why—why how ridiculous!"

"Yes'm, I s'pose it was. Missed him both times, too."

She called to Quong and he stopped wiping the stove long enough to turn his head.

"Quong, did somebody shoot at you?"

He looked fearfully toward the door and nodded violently.

"Yessash, two time. I go way bimeby. Too damn much shoot fo' me. Soup all gone; kittle busted. Hell's bells!"

"Quong!"

Hashknife laughed and went to the door, where he managed to retrieve the punctured kettle with a broom-handle. He dumped out the soup-bone, and with it came a battered piece of lead—the badly mushroomed bullet that had busted up Quong's soup.

Hashknife examined it closely and showed it to Quong.

"Looks like a thirty-thirty, Quong."

Calibers meant nothing in Quong's life, but he realized what that bullet would have done to him. Hashknife showed it to Miss Lanpher, but it failed to excite her in the least.

"Who would shoot at Quong?" she asked as if she did not believe it at all.

Quong turned quickly, a grin on his fat face.

"Mebbyso acclident. Somebody shoot clyote—bullet come heah. What you t'ink?"

"Now that's fine," laughed Hashknife. "I'll betcha that's it, Quong. Too bad it busted the kettle."

"You mean that they were shooting at something else and the bullet accidently came down here?" Thus Miss Lanpher, credulously.

"There's a lot of coyotes in the hills," said Hashknife, evading the direct question.

"There's some wolves and a lot of polecats, too, ma'am. I wish— say, Quong; has Trainor got a rifle here in the house?"

"Yessah. One rifle in room. I show you."

Quong trotted out and came back in a minute with a Winchester 45-70, which he handed to Hashknife, but Hashknife told him to take it back.

He had thought of going out into the hills and try to find the man who had fired the two shots, but decided that it would be a hopeless search.

Hashknife also knew that those shots were fired at him and not at the Chinese cook. He had been in line with Quong, who was in the shade and probably not visible to the man behind the rifle. From the reports of the gun, the man was shooting at extreme long range—and shooting only too well to suit Hashknife.

"They'll be dynamitin' the bunk-house next," mused Hashknife to himself, as Quong prepared the meal. "I've been lucky so far—but can it last?"

Miss Lanpher had retired to the front of the house, so Hashknife ate alone.

CHAPTER VII

IT WAS in the middle of the afternoon when Trainor, Mr. and Mrs. Lanpher and Poco Saunders came back from town. Hashknife did not go up to the house, but helped Poco unhitch the team. Poco was as uncommunicative as ever.

As they came out of the stable, Trainor was hobbling toward them, but stopped and called to Hashknife—

"What's this I hear about somebody shootin' at Quong?"

"Oh, that," Hashknife laughed and looked back toward the hills, "I reckon somebody was shootin' at coyotes. They came dam near hittin' the Chinaman, though. Lotsa folks are careless thataway."

"Uu-huh," Trainor grunted his unbelief. "Shootin' kinda high, wasn't they, Hartley?"

"Kinda."

"Say, do you really think they were shootin' at coyotes?"

"Well," smiled Hashknife, "that's all a matter of opinion. Mebbe the shooter felt thataway about it."

"Uh-huh, I see what yuh mean."

Trainor turned and went back to the house. Poco Saunders had heard the conversation, and now he turned and went into the bunkhouse ahead of Hashknife, who shut the door and faced him.

Poco's eyes narrowed, but he feigned not to notice Hashknife's steady gaze. Finally Hashknife said—

"Poco, I'll trade talk with yuh."

"Trade talk?" Poco did not seem to understand.

"Yeah. I was shot at twice this afternoon."

"I had nothin' to do with that, Hartley."

"Why do yuh tie yore gun to yuh at night, Poco?"

Poco started slightly, but his face did not betray that he was caught off his guard.

"Yore bunkie was shot from ambush, Poco," continued Hashknife. "Are you afraid of the same thing?"

Poco studied the question thoughtfully.

"Why should I be afraid?" he asked.

"I asked to trade talk—not to answer questions."

"Why should I trade talk? I know nothin'."

"All right."

Hashknife turned to his bunk, but stopped.

"Why did Pinto Cassidy draw a deadline between his place and the Circle Cross?"

"I don't know," replied Poco; and Hashknife felt that he was telling the truth.

"Are yuh afraid to talk about the rustlers who have been stealing stock on this range, Poco?"

"Why talk about 'em?"

"Well, for one reason is this—they've killed three men from ambush already."

"Three? You don't think that Ben Lanpher killed—"

Hashknife shook his head.

"Last night Jimmy, the half-breed; was shot in the arm, at the same spot where Smoky Cole was killed."

"He was?" Poco squinted thoughtfully, and Hashknife noticed that Poco's knuckles were white from their grip on his belt.

"Now, will yuh trade talk with me, Poco?"

But Poco shook his head slowly, his teeth shut tight.

"No, I can't trade a talk, because I know nothin'."

As Hashknife turned away, Buck Avery came in. He was half-drunk and was carrying a bottle in his hand, which he put under his pillow.

"Hyah, cowboys!" he greeted them. "Help yourself to the liquor. Reg'lar old poultry cocktail, that is. Six drinks and yuh lay. Hartley, yuh old son-of-a-gun, don't yuh never drink anythin'?"

But before Hashknife could reply, Trainor came to the door.

"Did you see old man Shappee, Buck?" he asked.

"Yeah; be right with yuh, Jim."

Buck kicked off his chaps, joined Trainor and they went toward the house together.

"Buck's drink in' too much," observed Poco. "He can't let it alone when he starts once. Trainor knows that, and he was a damn fool to start Buck off the other night."

"Trainor ain't picked another foreman yet, has he?" asked Hashknife casually.

"Nope. Prob'ly pick Buck, though. Buck has been with him ever since he took over the Circle Cross. Smoky and Buck came here together."

"How long you been here, Poco?"

"'Bout a year. Me and Smoky worked together before."

"Well, I'm not goin' to stay a year," laughed Hashknife. "There's too much promiscuous shootin' goin' on around here to suit me. Everybody's scared to talk for fear they're talkin' to the person who is doin' all the dirty work. It's a hell of a country, thasall."

"Yeah," nodded Poco solemnly. "I reckon that about describes it, Hartley."

Hashknife went outside and sat down on a bench beside the door. Buck was near the kitchen door, busy at the wash-bench and talking to Quong who was standing in the doorway. Miss Lanpher was out in the front yard, looking at a stunted rosebush, and Trainor was walking out to her.

She looked up, as he drew closer and seemed to be talking to her. For a few moments she listened to him; and then walked past him and into the house.

"He got froze up, too," chuckled Hashknife aloud.

"He sure did," agreed Poco, who had come to the door and noticed it.

"He's stuck on her pretty bad, I reckon. Anyway, he was kinda hard hit when she turned him down. I don't see nothin' to her m'self. Too danged high-toned. Tramor's a lot older than she is, and he ain't so damn handsome either."

"If she wants beauty I might stand a chance," laughed Hashknife.

"Yuh can't any more than get turned down."

"I've had mine, Poco."

Trainor walked around to the kitchen door and began talking to Buck, who threw his wash-pan of dirty water out on to the ground and slammed the pan viciously onto the bench.

They both seemed angry, but talked in low tones. Finally Buck whirled and came toward the bunk-house, swearing to himself. As he came up to the door he looked back toward the house, where Trainor was standing, looking toward them.

"I'll drink when and where I damn well please!" snarled Buck, and went into the bunk-house, where he, piled up on his bed and went to sleep.

That Buck had no respect for Trainor's authority was attested by the fact that Buck drank at intervals all night, and dug a fresh quart of liquor from beneath his straw tick the next morning.

He was incoherent in everything, except profanity, and refused to answer the breakfast call. Trainor's foot was much better, and he was jovial at breakfast.

"Hartley, you will go with Lanpher and me today. We're goin' to look over the range. Poco will drive the ladies to town."

"Somebody ought to stay with Buck," said Hashknife. "He's in bad shape."

"Let him sleep it off!" grated Trainor. "The fool won't let whisky alone; so he's the one to suffer."

They saddled their horses after breakfast and rode into the hills. Lanpher was unused to the saddle and knew little about riding, which handicapped them as far as speed was concerned.

They rode northeast almost to the main divide and swung around through the breaks, giving Lanpher some idea of what he owned. He had little to say, except in an undertone to Trainor. In fact, most of their conversation was handled in such a way that Hashknife was excluded.

Hashknife kept his eyes open and studied the country. On this side of the range there were few cattle of any brand, although there was plenty of water and feed. Hashknife remarked about it, but Trainor merely nodded and did not reply.

Lanpher looked queerly at Hashknife, as much as to say—

"You know the reason well enough."

Trainor had tied a lunch to the back of his saddle, and they ate at a spring far back in the hills. During the course of the lunch, Lanpher remarked—

"Carsten was in to see me not long ago, Jim."

"That so?"

"Yes. Just a friendly call, he said; but wanted to know what we had that was for sale."

"What did you tell him?"

"Well, I told him I didn't know. He said that beef was due to take a raise pretty soon. I'm not kicking on prices."

"No." Trainor shook his head. "We have no kick on the price of beef and hides."

They finished their lunch and mounted again. Hashknife grinned as Lanpher settled himself tenderly in the saddle and braced his feet solidly in the stirrups.

It was almost dark when they arrived at the ranch-house. Lanpher was thoroughly tired so Hashknife took care of the horse for him. Poco had just fed the wagon-team and told Hashknife that they had just arrived a short time before.

"What's new in Wolf Wells?" asked Hashknife.

"Nothin' much. I seen your pardner and the half-breed girl down there about noon. He's workin' at the Tomahawk, ain't he?"

"Well, I dunno about the work part of it," laughed Hashknife, as they entered the bunk-house.

Buck was still stretched out on the bunk and an empty bottle attested to the fact that Buck was "full as a tick." Poco tried to rouse him, but Buck refused to give more than a grunt.

Trainor ate supper with Hashknife and Poco, after the Lanpher family had eaten, and during the meal the sheriff and Lonesome Hobbs rode in. Hashknife saw them from the window, but said nothing. They dismounted and went to the front of the house.

"What's comin' off around here?" wondered Hashknife, as he saw three more riders ride down past the house and tie their horses to a corral fence.

He recognized one of them as being Ability Edwards. Trainor saw them, too, and hurriedly finished the rest of his meal. After he went out, Hashknife said to Poco:

"The sheriff and deputy came a few minutes ago, and just now, three more men rode in. What do yuh make of it?"

Poco halted with a cup at his lips, slowly placed it back in the saucer and got to his feet. He went to the door and looked out. Hashknife got up and went over to him.

The men had grouped a short distance from the porch and were talking as they looked down the road toward town. In a few moments three more riders appeared.

"That's Jud Carey, Bert Elhoff and Honey Simpson, all from the 66 outfit," said Poco. "Them first three are old man Shappee, Bility Edwards and Baldy Shannon, from the Flyin' M. I wonder what it means."

"Let's horn in and find out," grinned Hashknife.

The three riders dismounted and joined the group.

"Well, I reckon we're all here," observed Trainor, "so we might as well go into the house."

He led the way into the living-room and the men sat down on the chairs, or squatted on their heels against the wall. Lanpher had joined them at the door. Trainor glanced around at the group, but said nothing to Poco and Hashknife, who had invited themselves.

"Gentlemen," said Trainor seriously, "I reckon you all know why yo're here this evenin'. We've all suffered alike in this matter, and I think the time has come when we will have to step out into the open.

"Mr. Lanpher—" Trainor indicated him—"I reckon most of yuh met him when he was here before, and yuh know he is half-owner of the Circle Cross. He advised me to have yuh meet here and try to figure out some way to handle this proposition.

"I know how yuh feel about it. We've all been afraid to talk about it—or to do much. But I'll tell yuh it's comin' to a showdown. I don't mind tellin' yuh that the two men of mine that were killed were detectives; sent here by the association.

"Whether or not Smoky Cole was killed by the same gang, we don't know. I hope it can be proved on 'em. Yesterday two shots were fired from back there in the hills. One of 'em hit the casing of the kitchen door, while the other went into the kitchen and smashed into a kettle. Hartley, over there, was going toward the door at the time, and my cook was beside the doorway. I don't know which they were trying to kill."

The cattlemen considered this, as they looked at Hashknife and at each other. Old man Shappee, a typical old cattleman, cleared his throat raspingly.

"What did you ever do to 'em, Hartley?" he asked.

"It was kinda hard to tell—at that distance," grinned Hashknife, and the men smiled with him.

"Now, who has an idea to work on?" asked Trainor.

The men stirred uneasily. None of than seemed to want to commit themselves. Finally Jud Carey, a lanky, middle-aged man stood up.

"I dunno how anybody could figure out an idea," he drawled slowly. "It ain't like buckin' somethin' that yuh can see, Jim. The 66 has lost a lot of stock, but none of us has been shot at—yet."

He sat down slowly and lighted a cigaret.

"Aw, hell!" exploded Trainor. "Is everybody afraid to talk? Are we goin' to set here and shiver in our boots while a gang of bush-wackin' rustlers shoot our men from ambush and run off our stock?"

"All right—tell us what to do," suggested Shappee.

"Well," Trainor hesitated, "I'm damned if I know what to do. Lanpher and I have done what we think is the best thing; but we can't ask the association to send more men to the slaughter."

"How did this gang find out that they were detectives?" asked Bility Edwards.

"Nobody knows."

"They're sure a slick outfit," observed the sheriff. "I didn't know that these men were detectives. Nobody ever told me about 'em. One was killed near town and the other one on the Tomahawk ranch. It's almost a cinch that old Cassidy didn't kill both of 'em."

"Cassidy's a salty old son-of-a-gun, but I'll bet he never killed that feller," said Shappee, but qualified his statement with—

"Unless he's one of the gang himself."

"And that's what we don't know," said Trainor.

"Would it do you any good to make up a big posse and hunt every inch of the hills?" asked the sheriff.

"How would we know but what the men we're lookin' for would be ridin' along with us?" asked Carey.

"I dunno," said the sheriff foolishly.

"Well, anythin' is better than settin' around and bein' shot at, I should think," observed Shappee. "I'm ready to ride or do anythin' the majority wants to do."

"I wish I knew what to suggest." Thus William Lanpher, who had been a good listener.

"I have spent money for investigators, who have been killed. This is very unfortunate. I do not know how much stock you men have lost, but I do know that we have suffered severely. And, gentle-men, it is not going to stop, unless we are able to stop it."

"Yuh can't expect 'em to draw out of a cinch game, can yuh?" queried Bility Edwards.

"Why would they kill Smoky Cole?" demanded Lonesome, who had hardly spoken since he arrived.

"Smoky wasn't no detective."

"We don't know that they did," said Trainor, "but we hope it can be laid to their door so as to clear Ben Lanpher of the charge."

"Hell, he was too drunk to bushwhack anybody that day," declared Lonesome. "I reckon they done it."

"They're promiscuous all right," agreed Hashknife heartily. "Night before last they shot Jimmy Droop-drawers, the Tomahawk half-breed, while he was ridin' along the same place that Smoky Cole was killed."

"For gosh sake!" exploded Shappee, while the rest of them grunted or cursed in astonishment.

"You didn't tell me about this," said Trainor seriously.

Hashknife shook his head.

"No, I thought yuh had troubles enough, Trainor."

"Nobody told me," complained the sheriff. "Was he hurt much?"

Hashknife explained the extent of his injuries.

"And why did they try to kill the breed?" queried Lonesome dismally.

"My God, why don'tcha do somethin', except ask questions?" snorted the sheriff.

"Show me anybody that's doin' better than that," replied Lonesome. "I'm askin' damn pointed ones, y'betcha."

Lonesome's reply brought a grin, but it was short-lived.

Came the sound of a hurried footstep, the door was flung open and Lorna Cassidy almost fell inside the room. She shut the door behind her and stood with her back against it.

She was hatless, one sleeve of her dress was torn badly. Her hair was wind-blown and one of her long braids was wrapped once around her neck; as though she had ridden fast and far through the wind.

She looked from face to face in that smoke-fogged room, her lips shut tight, her eyes blazing, until she caught sight of Hashknife, and spoke directly to him.

"Your pardner was shot—hour—or—so—ago!" she panted.

Hashknife sprang to his feet, as did the rest of the men.

"My pardner—Sleepy. Shot? Not dead?"

She shook her head, her eyes still searching the room.

"No, not dead; hurt bad."

Hashknife went to her and took her by the arm.

"Don't hurry," he advised her hoarsely. "Take yore time and tell us all about it."

She nodded, leaning against the door, as she looked from face to face. She appeared to be looking for some one.

"We were out riding," she said slowly. "We had been to town and when we were coming back we decided to take a ride into the hills.

"We saw a man riding alone, but paid no attention to him. As we were riding down to our ranch, a shot was fired and my horse fell. I hurt my head a little, and before I could get up another shot was fired and Sleepy fell off his horse.

"I got him to the house and—" she shook her head wearily— "My mother helped me. She heard the shots, too."

"But how bad is he hurt?" asked Hashknife.

"I don't know. The bullet struck him under the left arm and knocked him off the horse. He didn't know anything for a while, but he woke up all right."

"How long ago did this happen?" asked Trainor.

"Oh, I don't know. It was a while before dark."

"And he hasn't had a doctor?" queried Hashknife.

Lorna shook her head.

"My mother is better than a doctor. She knows what to do. He knew I came over to tell you, and he said to tell you that he's all right."

"And you didn't see the man that fired the shots?" said the sheriff.

Lorna looked around the circle again and back at the sheriff.

"Yes, I seen him."

"Yuh did? My gosh! Who was he?"

"I got up, after my horse fell with me. I was dizzy for a minute, but I looked back toward the hill and I seen the man riding away. It was the same man we saw a while before."

"But who was he?" urged half-a-dozen voices, as the cattlemen crowded around her.

"Give us his name," demanded the sheriff.

But Lorna shook her head.

"No, not yet."

"Why not?"

"I told Sleepy about it and he said for me to not tell anybody."

"Well, that's a hell of a note!" wailed Lonesome.

Hashknife smiled grimly. He knew that Sleepy, even though badly hurt, knew that this information would be for them alone.

"You want to be party to a crime?" queried the sheriff. "If yuh don't tell, yo're as guilty as the shooter."

Lorna backed against the door and looked defiantly at him.

"All right, arrest me."

"Oh hell!"

The sheriff turned appealingly to the men.

"What can yuh do in a case like that?"

Hashknife turned and went out through the kitchen, heading for the barn. He saddled and led his horse outside, where he found the cattlemen waiting for him. Poco brushed past him, saying that he and Trainor were going along.

Lorna was already in the saddle; so he rode in beside her and they led the way. There was little conversation. Every man felt that they would soon know the name of the man who had been terrorizing the Ghost Hills Range, and they also knew that he would never live to be tried by a court of law.

Hashknife did not question Lorna, and he felt that these men would have their ride in vain. If Sleepy did not want her to tell the name of the killer, it was because this information might serve them to uncover the whole band.

Near the forks of the road he asked if it might not be well to send one man after the doctor at Wolf Wells, but she said:

"My mother good doctor. She knows what to do."

Hashknife knew that many of the Indians were adept at treating gunshot wounds, and a rangeland doctor is not usually a surgeon; so he agreed that her idea was probably the best.

It was a silent group of riders that dismounted at the open door of the Tomahawk ranch-house and filed inside. Sleepy was stretched out on a cot and beside him sat the Indian woman, Mrs. Cassidy.

Sleepy was very white, but he grinned at Hashknife and looked around at the crowd.

"Pardner, how do yuh feel?" asked Hashknife softly.

"Fine." Sleepy's voice was weak. "They come danged near handin' me a harp, Hashknife."

"Where did it hit yuh?"

"Kinda under the pit of m' arm and come out over m' chest. It sure ripped out hell of me. I must have cast-iron ribs, 'cause she didn't go inside."

"Then yuh ain't hurt bad." There was a note of relief in Hashknife's voice.

"F'r a minute I thought yuh was dead, cowboy."

"You didn't have nothin' on me. I seen seven flocks of angels flyin' in a V-shape over me. I says to myself, 'Sleepy, yo're goin' to be a migratory bird, instead of a harpist.'"

The sheriff shoved his way to the front and looked down at Sleepy.

"The girl says that yuh know who shot yuh."

Sleepy squinted up at the sheriff in amazement. He turned his head slowly and looked at the ring of faces around him.

"Well, I know that somebody did," he said softly, "but a feller with his face in the dust can't hardly see behind him and up a hill."

"But you seen the same feller before today," persisted the sheriff. "By God, we want to know who it was!"

"So do I," said Sleepy. "I want to be sure."

"You give us his name and we'll find out for yuh," stated old man Shappee.

Sleepy shook his head and looked appealingly at Hashknife, who turned to the crowd.

"Gents, yuh can't bother him no more now. He's been bad hurt, and he don't want to talk."

The crowd moved back to the doorway and the Indian woman sat down beside Sleepy, giving him a drink of something that had a most peculiar odor.

There was no question but what the cattlemen were not in the best of humor. They had come a long way after information and had not received it.

"I don't understand why they won't talk," said Trainor. "This ain't a thing to keep secret. If the guilty one finds out that they are known, they'll fog out of the country and we'll never see 'em again."

"Well," Lonesome shook his head sadly, "that sure wouldn't hurt my feelin's, none whatever. They can't fog too soon nor too far to suit old man Hobbs' little son."

"Damn it!" wailed the sheriff dismally. "What's the good of havin' a sheriff."

"I've argued the same question many times," smiled Hashknife, "but yuh never can make folks listen to reason. I never seen one yet that was good for anythin', except pitchin' horseshoes."

"What I want to know is this." Jud Carey spat dryly and looked around. "When do we git informed as to who the shooter was?"

"Don't look at me!" snapped the sheriff. "I've asked questions until m' tonsils are all raw. I don't see why they're keepin' this to themselves, danged if I do."

"I reckon there's nothin' to be learned here," said Shappee wearily, "and it's a long ride back to the old Flyin' M. I ain't as young as I used to be."

"Come over and stay with us tonight," offered Trainor.

"Yeah, and have ma pawin' holes in the carpet, 'cause I don't come home. She's scared stiff, jist thinkin' that I might git shot in the back. I told her that at my age it didn't make a damn bit of difference whether they shot me in the back or the front. I'm much obliged to yuh, just the same, Trainor."

"You're sure welcome to come," laughed Trainor, and turned to Hashknife.

"You goin' back with us, Hartley?"

Hashknife shook his head quickly.

"No, I reckon I'll stay here tonight. Mebbe I'll have to go after a doctor, but I don't think so. Anyway, I'll be over early in the mornin'."

They went back to their horses and rode away down the moonlit highway, which wound in and out of the brushy cañons. Hashknife watched them until they faded out in the distance, and turned back, closing the door behind him.

He crossed the room and drew the blanket curtain across the window near the cot. Lorna had sat down near the fireplace, and a moment later Jimmy, the half-breed, slipped in the front door and closed it quickly.

Jimmy was carrying a shotgun, which he leaned against the wall. The squaw spoke to him in the Sioux tongue and he shook his head.

"Lorna go way, Jimmy watch," volunteered the squaw in explanation.

"See nothin'," grunted Jimmy, coming closer to the cot and grinning at Sleepy.

"You feel good, eh? Minnie damn good doctor."

Hashknife walked over and squatted down on his heels beside the cot.

"Yuh want to talk about it, Sleepy?" he asked.

"Ask Lorna."

Lorna came closer and spoke softly.

"It was Buck Avery."

"Buck Avery?"

Hashknife squinted thoughtfully. Buck had been drunk for two days. He was still drinking that morning, and was dead drunk just before supper.

"I'm sorry, but I reckon yuh made a mistake, Lorna," he said slowly, and told them of Buck's drinking.

"I told her not to tell anybody, and I'm glad she didn't," said Sleepy weakly. "It don't pay to be too quick in a thing like that."

Lorna shook her head slowly and stared at the blank wall.

"No talk much," grunted the squaw, "damn good thing."

"I seen that man," persisted Lorna, as if visualizing him now. "He rode like Buck Avery and he looked like Buck Avery. But this man was not drunk."

"Got me the second shot," grinned Sleepy. "His first one must 'a' just grazed me and hit Lorna's horse in the head. No drunken man fired them two shots."

"Which lets Buck out," declared Hashknife. "He's been drunk ever since I went to the Circle Cross. But this sure puts us in one fine fix. The guilty party will think that we know 'em, and they'll either pull out of the country or try harder to wipe us out."

"Don't worry sick man," advised the squaw. "Go to bed."

"That's good advice," admitted Hashknife, and to Sleepy—

"If that bullet tore yuh up bad, suppose I go after a doctor and have him sew yuh up."

"I fixum," grunted the squaw. "No need doctor."

"That's a cinch," grinned Sleepy. "Mother fixed me up fine. I couldn't be sewed tighter if they used a sewing-machine on me. Don'tcha bother about me, Hashknife; you keep yore own skin together."

Hashknife accepted a blanket from Lorna, kicked off his boots and rolled up in a corner. He was dog-tired, but his mind refused to rest. He wondered who rode and looked like Buck Avery.

Mentally he compared every Ghost Hills cowpuncher that he knew, but none of them looked like Buck. Still, at a distance, there was a similarity between Buck and Honey Simpson, the silent puncher from the 66. Even Bility Edwards might be mistaken for Buck.

But his mind always jerked back to Buck Avery, snoring on the bunk, with the empty bottle beside him and the bunk-house smelling strongly of liquor. Buck was drunk the night that Jimmy, the half-breed, had been shot, and Buck had gone to the Flying M ranch at the time that Quong had nearly been hit.

The Flying M was west of the Circle Cross, while the shots had been fired from the east. Buck had been to Wolf Wells that day, and had also carried the message to the Flying M for Trainor.

And last, but not least, there was not a .30-30 rifle on the Circle Cross. The bullet that wrecked Quong's kettle was a .30-30. Hashknife had seen Smoky Cole's wound, but it was hard to tell what kind of a bullet had killed him. He wished now that he had examined it more closely.

He resolved to examine the dead horse in the morning and see if he could find the bullet. Lorna was sitting by the fireplace, her chin cupped in her hands and Hashknife studied her profile.

Just beyond her, and to the right, sat her mother, a short, squat, typical Indian woman. He thought of Pinto Cassidy, with his wizened, wrinkled, Irish countenance, and wondered what freak of nature had given these two an offspring like Lorna. She was as unlike either of them as a child could be.

And then he went to sleep to dream of miles of mesquite clumps with a bushwhacker behind each one, and him with a .45-70 rifle and nothing to shoot in it, except .30-30 caliber cartridges.

Just after midnight a severe thunderstorm swept the Ghost Hills, and the downpour of rain thudded hollowly On the roof of the Tomahawk ranch-house; but Hashknife slept the sleep of the just, in spite of it all.

It was barely past daylight when Hashknife awoke and rolled out of his blanket. The old squaw was already preparing breakfast and Sleepy was snoring soundly. Jimmy, the half-breed, put in a yawning appearance, and peered cautiously out of a window.

"Whatcha see?" queried Hashknife.

"I just look," replied Jimmy.

"Uh-huh."

Hashknife rolled a cigaret and turned to the squaw.

"Mother, how's the patient gettin' along?"

She smiled widely and nodded toward the cot.

"He get well now—pretty quick."

"He sure didn't git hit in his snoser," grinned Hashknife, and nodded to Lorna who had just come in.

She walked over, looked at Sleepy, who awoke and grinned up at her.

"How are yuh feelin', cowboy?" asked Hashknife.

"Finer 'n frawg-hair. Gimme a cigaret."

They sat down and discussed the happenings of the evening before, but Lorna still persisted that the man looked exactly like Buck Avery.

"But," argued Hashknife, "Buck has been drunk for several days. He was drunk when we found him yesterday."

"Lorna know Buck pretty good," said Jimmy.

"All right," grinned Hashknife. "If it was Buck, he's headin' out of this country right now. He'd hear that Lorna seen him, and he'd sure fade away fast. But where would Buck fit into the scheme of things?"

No one seemed to have an answer for that question. They ate breakfast and Hashknife announced his intentions of going back to the Circle Cross ranch.

"No damn good," declared Jimmy.

"Yuh think they'd bushwhack me, Jimmy?"

"Think plenty now," advised Jimmy.

Hashknife grinned and puffed on his cigaret.

"Mebbe yo're right, Jimmy," he finally agreed. "They'd hate to have me pack information back with me, I reckon. None of 'em know the name that Lorna had in mind, but they'd know clanged well that I'd have it now. Mebbe we better try somethin' easy at first."

Hashknife selected an old pair of overalls, an old shirt and a pair of boots. Three blankets sufficed for the stuffing of them. He tied a rope around the dummy under the arms and left a length of rope extending from each side. Then he surmounted the thing with his own hat, fitting it to the roll of blanket which extended up through the neck of the shirt.

"Grab hold of a rope, Jimmy," he ordered, and the half-breed obeyed with a grin.

"Looks more like me than I do," laughed Hashknife as he dragged the dummy over to the door.

"Now, Jimmy, you stand on one side and hold yore rope high and tight enough to make the darned things stand up like a man. Don't expose yourself, young feller. All set?"

Jimmy nodded and drew the rope tight. Hashknife looked back in the room to see that nothing was in line. Then he shoved the door wide open. The dummy looked like a cowboy. Perhaps it was a trifle limp-looking at close range.

It stood there for perhaps five seconds motionless. Then it jerked convulsively and fell sidewise. From the rear of the roam came the splat of a bullet striking wood, and from the hills came the thin pop of a high-power cartridge.

Hashknife reached out and drew the door shut. Jimmy stood there, looking foolishly at a piece of rope in his hand, which had been cleanly severed. It was a rope made from Maguey fiber, about the size of a clothes-line, but very hard and brittle.

"Well," said Hashknife, shoving the dummy aside, "I'll say that it worked to the queen's taste."

The two women were staring wonderingly at him, but Sleepy was laughing joyously. Jimmy crossed the room and poked his finger at the spot where the bullet had bored into the seasoned wall.

"We're sure hived up for keeps," said Sleepy, as if rather pleased at the prospect. Sleepy loved a fight, and nothing pleased him more than to give odds.

"You ain't in it, you doggone cripple," reminded Hashknife. "Yuh don't need to start cheerin' about it."

Jimmy had moved the curtain an inch and was staring out through the window.

"See anythin'?" asked Hashknife.

"Nothin'. They think you dead—mebbe."

"Very likely. But they won't stop at one killin'. They will naturally think that we all know the guilty man, acid they'll try to stop all of us. You got a rifle, Jimmy?"

"You damn right!"

Jimmy went into another room and came back with an old .50-90 Sharps, which he handled lovingly before giving it to Hashknife.

"That good-gun, you bet."

Hashknife grinned and examined it. He knew the killing power of the old Sharps, even though they did not compare with the high-power rifle. He accepted a handful of cartridges from the half-breed.

"Whatcha goin' to do?" queried Sleepy anxiously.

"I'm goin' into the hills," grinned Hashknife. "I'm goin' to have a perfectly good little fight, and yo're goin' to lay here in yore nice little beddie and wish you was along; sabe?"

"Aw hell! You'll go out there and get yore danged hide all filled up with soft-nose bullets that's what you'll do. Ain'tcha got no sense, Hashknife?"

"Sour grapes," retorted Hashknife, and to Jimmy—

"Gimme more shells."

Jimmy gave him several more, which Hashknife pocketed. He rescued his hat from the dummy and drew it tightly on his head.

"Now, you folks just set tight, will yuh? I've got to teach them bushwhackers that they ain't got the only rifle in the Ghost Hills. Adios. That means good-by in Spanish."

"Thirty-thirty," retorted Sleepy. "That means good-by in any darned language."

Hashknife went to the rear of the house, opened a window as wide as possible, stood up on a chair and fairly dived outside. He landed on his feet, ducked low and ran swiftly toward the upper corral, running in a zigzag angle to confuse any one who might be trying to use him for a target.

He had almost reached the angle of the corral fence when—

Whim-m-m-m!

A bullet tore up the ground almost under his feet and zee-e-e-e'd its way up the slope of the hills. It was too close for comfort, and Hashknife was thankful for the protection of a patch of brush behind the corral fence.

"Good shootin'," he panted aloud, as he crawled like a snake fifty feet from where he had dropped behind the brush.

The shooter was evidently unable to determine just where Hashknife had gone; so he tore a few splinters off the pole-corral, just taking a chance on scoring a hit.

Hashknife worked his way the length of the corral and into a bunch of brush on the side of the hill, where he snuggled into a depression and prayed for a chance to do a little shooting. He studied the hills beyond the ranch-house, but could see nothing.

He knew that the man had not seen him take cover on the hill, because no more shots had been fired. He had watched closely for about five minutes, when his vigilance was rewarded.

Something moved in a jumble of brush and rocks, but the distance was a good four hundred yards. It moved again, and this time Hashknife could see that it was a man. He appeared to be moving very slowly, and was evidently trying to work his way higher in order to get a better view beyond the corral fence.

Hashknife estimated the distance and set his sights. It was a long shot and a small target, as the man did not expose much of his anatomy at a time.

The old gun kicked viciously and emitted a cloud of smoke; while its report clattered like artillery, as it echoed from the surrounding hills.

Hashknife ducked low under the smoke and saw the bullet strike. It threw up a cloud of dust about a foot below where the target had been.

"Next time, brother," promised Hashknife, as he shoved in another cartridge.

But the next moment a bullet splattered into the bank behind him, causing him to hug the ground tightly. Another struck to his left, another to his right. The man was trying to find out his location.

Another bullet ricocheted off a rock behind him, while the next one threw sand in his face.

Hashknife snorted loudly, kicked himself loose from that location and rolled back down the hill, where he scuttled up the draw a little and got behind a big rock.

"That danged old smoke-wagon sure advertised my location," he panted aloud. "Anyway, I scared him so that he wasn't exactly sure just where I was."

He stayed flat on the ground and re covered his breath, while an occasional bullet searched along the corral fence, but did no damage. He knew that the man had not seen him take cover so he felt reasonably safe.

But inaction soon palled upon him and he looked around for a good place to try for again. Just to the left of the corral was a jumble of broken rock and a clump of greasewood, which would make a fine breastworks. It was about a hundred feet away, but Hashknife took the chance and ran for it. He fell in behind the grease-wood, without a shot being fired.

"That's danged funny," he told himself. "What's happened to m' friend with the .30-30?"

There was no question but what the man could have seen him make the run. He studied the spot where the man had been, but there was nothing there as far as he could see.

"Gotta make him start somethin'," he told a lone magpie, which had stopped on a tall post and was chattering angrily over something.

Hashknife drew his feet under him, gripped the rifle tightly and ran for the corner of the barn like a rabbit hunting a hole. But there was no response from the man on the hill. He crawled in through a broken window and secured a saddle-blanket, which he hung on a pitchfork and tried to draw a shot by extending it slightly past the corner of the barn.

Then he walked deliberately into the open and headed for the house. But no shots were fired at him.

"Somethin' chased him away, I reckon," he decided, as he went back into the house.

Lorna and Jimmy met him at the door while Sleepy yelled weakly for details of the slaughter.

"I shot at him once and scared him away," laughed Hashknife.

"Don't lie to a cripple," wailed Sleepy.

"Well, he just quit shootin' then," grinned Hashknife. "Somethin' scared him away, and I'm going to see if I can find out what it was. I'll be back this evenin'."

"I'm goin' to get up tomorrow," declared Sleepy hopefully, looking at the old squaw.

"I ain't sick, am I, mother?"

"You pretty good. Get up bimeby."

"Yuh betcha. I can ride and shoot as good as ever and I'm danged if I'm goin' to let you have all the fun."

Hashknife laughed teasingly.

"Sleepy, I sure had fun. That son-of-a-gun seen the smoke from this old rifle and he sure salivated everythin' in range. Powee-e-e-e! Bullets everywhere, and me down in a little swale, with m' stummick wrapped around my vertebray. Ha, ha, ha, ha, ha!"

Sleepy swore softly at anybody lucky enough to have fun like that, and Hashknife went swiftly down to the barn and saddled his horse. Jimmy, the half-breed, had put up the horse the night before. Hashknife still kept the Sharps rifle, and rode away with it across the fork of his saddle.

He pointed straight into the hills to the spot where the man had been hiding. The downpour of rain the night before had softened the ground a little, and Hashknife was able to find where the man's heels had dug into the dirt.

He trailed the man to the top of the hogback, but there he was forced to give up the scent. Greasewood and tall sage grew in profusion on this hog-back, and the man had evidently taken advantage of it, as the last tracks that Hashknife had found were pointing up the slope.

He mounted again and followed the ridge, watching closely. He rode around the heads of several brushy coulées and was about to head back toward the road, when he spied a rider crossing the coulée below him. Hashknife dropped off his horse and watched closely. The rider went slowly up the side of the hill, going cautiously and scanning the country carefully.

"Poco Saunders," muttered Hashknife, as he adjusted his sights carefully. "Poco, yo're coyote bait right now."

But something in Poco's actions caused him to hold his fire. He was leaning down from his saddle, as if searching for something on the ground. He rode ahead a short distance and from his actions it seemed that he was following a trail.

Hashknife squatted low in the brush and watched him reach the ridge and disappear over the other side.

"Now that's a queer actin' jasper," Hashknife told his horse. "Mebbe we better see what's ailin' him."

He circled the head of the coulée and picked up Poco's horse-tracks. He waited a while and finally he saw Poco far down the next coulée, heading along the side of it, still looking down.

Hashknife looked closely down at the horse-tracks and discovered that two horses had passed that way.

"Poco's trailin' somebody, and I'm trailin' him," he laughed. "Kinda like button, button, who's got the button."

He gave Poco plenty of time to get out of sight before he took up the trail again, which kept bearing toward the road. Finally he reached the top of the hill, where he could look down at the road, but the trail did not lead directly down.

He could see where Poco had started down, lost the trail and had come back to the top again. The trail led along the top for possibly an eighth of a mile, as if the rider had been looking over the country below, and headed down a heavily wooded coulée, which opened into a little swale down near the road.

At the lower end of the open swale was a clump of old cottonwoods, and it was near these that the trail practically ended. Here were the marks of footprints, as if the horse had stood there several minutes.

"Heard somebody comin' along the road," decided Hashknife, as he went on down to the road, where all the footprints jumbled into those of the regular country traffic.

Hashknife noted that he had struck the road just below where the road forked to the Circle Cross ranch; so he swung to the east and rode slowly through the hills to the ranch.

He wondered what Poco was doing in the hills and who he was trailing.

"Was Poco doin' the shootin'?" he wondered. "Did somebody scare him and was he trailin' this other party to see what they were up to? Or did Poco happen in, hear the shots and start trailin' the shooter?"

As far as he could see, Poco carried no rifle; but at that distance it would not be possible to see whether there might be one in a scabbard on the saddle.

"Anyway," he decided as he rode in at the ranch, "the shooter got scared and pulled out. They may be goshawful bad, but they can be scared, that's a cinch."

CHAPTER VIII

HE PUT up his horse and went up to the house, where he found Buck Avery eating breakfast. Buck looked unkempt and appeared to be still shaky from drink.

"'Lo, Hartley," he grunted, helping himself to more black coffee. "They tell me yore friend got shot yesterday. How's he gittin' along?"

"Fine, Buck. Didn't hurt him much, and he'll be out right away."

"Tha's good," mumbled Buck. "Had yore breakfast?"

"Yeah, long time ago."

"Time f'r another. Hey! Quong! Fry the gent some aigs."

"Yessah, lite away."

Hashknife did not object. He was always in the mood for ham and eggs, and it had been two hours or more since he had eaten.

"Where's Trainor?" asked Hashknife.

"Gone t' town with Lanpher. Poco went over to the Tomahawk t' see how yore friend is. Didn't yuh meet him?"

Hashknife shook his head and attacked his eggs.

"No. I came across the hills."

"Uh-huh."

Buck gulped his coffee and began rolling a cigaret.

"I'm off the hooch," he declared. "I've seen a whole danged mee-nag-i-ree pee-radin' around here the last two days. Caught me two vi'let colored elephants las' evenin', but they gnawed their way out of the corral."

He got up rather unsteadily and headed for the bunk-house. Hashknife laid aside his knife and fork. Something caused him to distrust Buck, although he could not see how Buck could have done all the deviltry. He sauntered out and went down to the barn, where he examined Buck's horse, but there was nothing to show that the animal had been ridden that day. It was true that Buck could have removed all traces of travel; but the animal's spirits did not fit in with a fifteen-mile trip.

"If he rode yuh today, he didn't ride yuh far," declared Hashknife, and went outside where he sat down on an old lumber-pile and grew comfortable over his cigaret.

Mrs. Lanpher came out on the porch of the ranch-house and Hashknife mentally compared her and her daughter to Mrs. Cassidy, the squaw, and Lorna.

"Too much money and too much convention," decided Hashknife. "They ain't a danged bit natural. Still, they're mothers, just the same—and this one's got a boy in jail."

He sauntered up to the porch and was surprized to receive a cordial "good-morning" from Mrs. Lanpher.

"Sure is a nice mornin', ma'am," admitted Hashknife, sitting down on the steps. "How's all yore folks?"

"Mr. Lanpher has gone to town with Mr. Trainor and Helen has a slight headache," she replied.

"What is the latest news from your friend who was hurt last night?"

"Thank yuh kindly, ma'am; he's doin' fine. He got kinda ripped up a little, thasall."

"I am very glad to hear he is doing so well. I asked my husband to explain some of these things to me last night, and what he told me was surprizing, to say the least. Why the whole country must be in a turmoil. And nobody knows who is doing it all."

"No, ma'am, they sure don't. Yore husband and Trainor are doin' everythin' they can, I reckon."

She nodded slowly, thoughtfully.

"I know little about these things, but it seems that the loss in stock has been tremendous. But—" she stared across the gray hills and her lips twitched slightly— "I—I would not mind it—the money part of it—if my boy was back with us again."

"Yes'm, that part of it is kinda hard," agreed Hashknife. "I'd sure like to help him, ma'am. But you've sure got to take him away from the range country, when he gets loose.

"Yore boy is all right, ma'am; he's fine, inside. But he got a lot of queer notions, don'tcha know it? Somebody told him that he was a good shot, and he immediate and soon proclaims himself a gunman and goes seekin' a victim.

"He got to likin' whisky, too. It's bad for kids, ma'am. Ben's all right, and I don't want yuh to think that I'm paintin' him worse than I ought to. Yessir, he's all right."

"Thank you, Mr. Hartley," she said softly. "I feel that you know my boy well enough to express an opinion. We have been lax with him, I know. Mr. Lanpher was not at all discreet in the matter of his—er—feelings toward the half-breed girl. Of course it was absurd for Ben to think of such an alliance, but it might have been handled differently."

"Well," Hashknife settled himself and began rolling a cigaret carefully. "Well, ma'am, there's a lot worse things could happen to Ben. Half-breeds don't make bad wives. I 'member that old Jake Dickson married one over in the Button Wilier country, and she stood for old Jake two years before she killed him in a friendly fight.

"And there was old 'Shep' Hardy, over in the Skiwaumpus country. He married a breed girl. Everybody said that ho human could get along with old Shep for thirty days; but she was ca'm and patient with him—which no white woman would have been—and he annoyed her for darned near a year before she stole the ladder out of his prospect shaft and left him there, while she run away with a sheepherder. I tell yuh, they're fine wives, if yuh give 'em a chance, ma'am."

"Horrors!" Mrs. Lanpher shuddered visibly.

"Of course," amended Hashknife, "he ain't got her yet, and he may not be lucky enough to get her; but she's a fine girl."

"But to think of Benjamin Lanpher marrying an Indian! Why, it would never do at all, don't you see."

"She sure's got ancestors," grinned Hashknife. "I heard a feller braggin' once about his ancestors comin' over in the Mayflower. Called his family old-timers. He sure paraded his great-grandpas, until a dark-complected gent spoke up and said that his folks was pretty good sort of folks, until that darned boat showed up.

"Come to find out, the dark-complected gent had a lot of Delaware Injun blood in him, and he proved to this Mayflower gent that his Injun ancestors were free as birds years before the Mayflower gent's ancestors quit bein' branded by their owners."

"I—I suppose that is true," agreed Mrs. Lanpher, "but that does not lessen the fact that we do not want Ben to marry this girl."

"All right," said Hashknife. "Neither do I, ma'am. Talkin' seriously, I don't like marriages of that kind. I've got a lot of respect for Injun blood, when it ain't been tainted. Mixin' Injun and white blood brings out the vices of both and the virtues of neither.

"Lorna is a doggoned sweet little girl—too sweet for yore son—the way he's been actin'. And I'm whisperin' my objections to this, here marriage as much for her sake as for Ben. She's got just as much right to be happy as he has, don't cha see? I reckon we all dislike to see 'em get married. Even Trainor don't like it."

"That is one of the reasons that Ben refused to stay here oh this ranch," explained Mrs. Lanpher. "Mr. Trainor knew what Ben was doing, so he wrote to us about it Ben resented it greatly and left the ranch."

"That was too bad," agreed Hashknife heartily.

"You've known Trainor a long time, ain't yuh, ma'am?"

"Mr. Lanpher has."

"Ma'am, I am goin' to ask yuh a personal question, if yuh don't mind."

Mrs. Lanpher looked curiously at him.

"A personal question?"

"Yes'm; I was goin' to ask yuh if yore daughter is goin' to marry Trainor?"

Mrs. Lanpher's lips shut tightly, but she smiled a trifle as she shook her head.

"No, I do not think so. Why do you ask that question?"

"Just kinda curious, thasall."

"No." Mrs. Lanpher shook her head and sighed deeply. "A year ago Helen was not of age, and Mr. Trainor wanted her to marry him. I refused, because I did not think that she knew her own mind in the matter. And more than that, Mr. Trainor is twice her age.

"No doubt Mr. Trainor would make a good husband; but with her advantages I think she could do much better. I explained it fully to Mr. Trainor and he was gentleman enough to—well, not exactly agree with me—but to drop the matter."

"What did Mr. Lanpher think of it?" asked Hashknife.

"Well, he was not at all diplomatic. He said it was absurd—and I think he told Mr. Trainor just that."

Hashknife rubbed out his cigaret against the step and got to his feet. Poco Saunders was riding in through the main gate, heading for the barn. Hashknife turned to Mrs. Lanpher.

"Ma'am, I didn't mean to pry into yore family affairs, and I ask yore pardon. I'll sure do all I can to open the jail for yore boy."

"Thank you so much," she replied. "It was good to just have some one to talk to, and those family affairs are no secret."

Hashknife lifted his hat and went to the barn where Poco was unsaddling. He looked at Hashknife curiously, but said nothing as he hung up his saddle and came back to the door.

"I been out to the Tomahawk," volunteered Poco.

"Yeah, I seen yuh," replied Hashknife easily.

"Yuh did?" Poco squinted reflectively, thoughtfully.

"Yuh did?" He repeated the question. "Where?"

"Back in the hills," Hashknife was watching Poco closely, but he was relaxed, as he leaned against the door.

"Back in the hills, eh?" Softly.

"Uh-huh," Hashknife took a deep breath and hooked his thumbs over his belt.

"Poco Saunders, we're goin' to trade talk this time."

Poco looked up quickly, but there was no anger, no defiance in his dark eyes.

"We're goin' to trade talk," said Hashknife, "and yo're goin' to talk first, Poco."

Poco nodded slowly and a bitter smile flashed across his thin lips, as he said—

"Where do I begin, Hartley?"

"Start in with this mornin', Poco."

"We got up early this mornin', Hartley. After breakfast, me and Lanpher and Trainor started for town. Trainor's got an idea of foller-in' the sheriff's idea of makin' up a big posse. We got almost to town and they got to talkin' about Stevens gettin' shot. Kinda wonderin' how he is, yuh know, and they decided that I'm to ride back to the Tomahawk ranch and see how hings are goin'.

"I'm to tell you that they're goin' to make up this big posse, and then I might as well go back to the ranch. Lanpher gets to kinda worryin' about the women bein' alone, and all that. I rides back and I'm almost to the—"

"What time did yuh leave the ranch?" interrupted Hashknife.

"I dunno. It wasn't much after daylight. Why?"

"Go ahead."

"Like I just said, I'm almost to the Tomahawk, when I hears a shot. I stops and considers things. Mebbe I'm there live or ten minutes, when there's more shootin'. I mosey on up the road, and I'm almost to the ranch, when I see the shooter. He's quite a ways from me, but I think he seen me at the same time Anyway, he ducks real rapid.

"I take things kinder easy, and foller him. That rain made the ground kinda soft and I'm able to trail him, but it only winds through the hills and comes back to the road. Then I go back to the Tomahawk and find you gone. Anythin' else?"

"Only to say that you told the truth, Poco. Do you want to ask me any questions?"

Poco considered deeply for a while, and then—

"Who are you, Hartley?"

"Cowpuncher," grinned Hashknife. "Just a puncher."

"Uh-huh. Why is somebody tryin' to kill you?"

Hashknife scratched his head thoughtfully.

"Poco, I can't tell yuh, because I ain't sure. Yuh see, they ain't never told me why. Mebbe I've got my own ideas on the subject, but a feller is liable to figure things a little wrong."

Poco nodded thoughtfully, his eyes squinted. Hashknife studied him for a moment and then—

"Poco, I forgot to ask yuh one question."

"Thasso? What is it?" Pocco did not look up.

"You asked me who I am—who are you?"

"Me?" Poco's thin lips fluttered in a bitter laugh. "I'm a damn fool, I reckon."

Hashknife laughed and slapped hin on the back.

"Poco, we all are, but we're just as happy as though we had good sense. I hate to pry into anybody's private affairs, but I'd sure like to know why Smoky held out to try and convict old Pinto Cassidy."

"Don't you think he's guilty?" queried Poco.

"No—do you?"

"I did," said Poco shortly, and after a few moments of reflection—

"He threatened to kill any Circle Cross puncher that trespassed on the Tomahawk."

"Why?"

"I told yuh once that I didn't know why, Hartley. But I think it was on account of the half-breed girl."

Poco turned away and headed for the bunk-house, while Hashknife sat down beside the barn in the shade, and watched Poco go jerkily along on his high-heeled boots.

"You've got an ax to grind, but I don't think yuh know where to find the grindstone," observed Hashknife to himself. "I'd rather have yuh on my side than against me, 'cause, you come nearer bein' a cold-blooded gunman than anybody I've seen for quite a while."

Hashknife had never seen Poco Saunders in trouble, but he felt instinctively that Poco would be swift with a gun. Every motion betokened the gunman; cool, calculating, sober and unemotional.

Hashknife felt sure that Poco had been greatly affected by the murder of Smoky Cole, his bunkie. There was no doubt that Poco did not know who had killed Smoky, but that Poco was trying hard to find out.

Poco had used the past tense in speaking of his opinion of Cassidy's guilt, and Hashknife wondered whether the recent bushwhacking had convinced Poco that both Cassidy and Ben Lanpher were innocent.

"Well, we're earnin' that Lanpher money that's a cinch," observed Hashknife. "This kind of a job needs armor more than it does brains."

* * * *

He got to his feet as Trainor, Lanpher and a third man rode in through the big gate, and waited for them to come to the barn. It was not until this third man dismounted that Hashknife recognized him as being Carsten, the cattle-buyer, whom he and Sleepy had met at Lanpher's house in San Francisco.

Both Trainor and Lanpher spoke to Hashknife, but Carsten did not even look at him.

"Hartley, will yuh take care of the horses?" asked Trainor, Handing Hashknife his reins.

Hashknife nodded and collected the three sets of reins.

"We'll go up to the house," said Trainor, and he and Carsten started away.

Lanpher stooped to take off his spurs and when he stood up, the other two were half-way to the house.

"I got Carsten aside and told him not to recognize you," explained Lanpher hurriedly "I didn't want even Trainor to know that Carsten met you."

"That's the stuff," grinned Hashknife, but added, "Even if everybody else seems to know what we're tryin' to do here."

"It must be only the guilty ones, though," protested Lanpher quickly. "We had a talk with the sheriff and he plans a big sweep of the whole country very soon. How is Stevens?"

"He's doin' fine. That squaw sure beats the doctors."

Lanpher frowned slightly, but a glad smile chased it away immediately, as he said:

"Hartley, my boy gets his trial day after tomorrow. We were notified of it today. Mitchell, the San Francisco lawyer, will defend him. He gets his trial even ahead of Cassidy's second one.

"Mitchell is optimistic, but admits that the evidence is greatly against us. In fact—" Lanpher's eyes were wistful and his voice broke slightly— "In fact, we haven't any evidence in our favor, except Ben's unsupported word. He—he had been rather wild, I am told, and that will all be against him; but my boy did not commit murder, Hartley."

Hashknife shook his head in agreement and turned to the barn door with the horses.

"No, I don't reckon he did. Ben was just a plumb damn fool, thasall. He's got a hard, hard fight ahead of him, Lanpher, and some of them recent wild oats are goin' to make all of yuh sick of the lad's sowin'. But you stick with him.

"That prosecutin' attorney is sure goin' to hang a red fringe around the kid, y'betcha. He'll make you think you raised a locoed bobcat instead of a boy; but don't mind him. He's paid to say nasty things about folks."

Lanpher nodded slowly, as he held out his hand to Hashknife.

"Hartley, I appreciate what you've said."

They shook hands solemnly and Lanpher went to the house, where Mrs. Lanpher and Helen were talking to Carsten and Trainor. Hashknife stabled the horses and went to the bunk-house, where he found Buck half-asleep on a bunk and Poco playing his interminable game of solitaire.

Hashknife told them that Lanpher and Trainor had returned, and mentioned the stranger, who limped slightly with his right leg.

"Kinda thin-faced?" asked Poco indifferently. "Little gray in his hair?"

"Uh-huh."

Buck cleared his throat huskily.

"Must be Carsten, Poco;" and to Hashknife:

"He's a cattle-buyer. Works for some Eastern outfit."

"Sets on a horse like a puncher," observed Hashknife.

Buck laughed.

"Oh, I reckon, Carsten ain't no tenderfoot. Feller's kinda got to sabe horses and cows, if he's goin' to mix with cattle-folks and buy their stock."

"Yeah, that's true," admitted Hashknife.

He sauntered outside and saddled his horse. Inaction palled upon him so he rode up past the ranch-house and told Trainor that he was going back to the Tomahawk. Trainor came down from the porch.

"Lanpher just told me that Stevens is gettin' along fine," he said. "We're glad to hear it. We talked with the sheriff today, and in a short time we are going to comb these hills so thoroughly that even a gopher will have to dig deep to keep out of our way.

"You go right ahead over to the Tomahawk and stay as long as yuh want to. Mr. Carsten, a cattle-buyer, will be here for a few days, and I will likely be busy with him. Ben Lanpher's trial comes up Wednesday; so his father will likely be busy with the lawyer. Poco and Buck can take care of everything."

He glanced down toward the bunk-house, and added—

"If Buck will try and stay sober."

"I reckon he's sick of liquor," grinned Hashknife.

"By God, I hope so! He ain't got no judgment Well, so-long, and good luck."

Trainor had been drinking a little—just enough to put him in rare good humor, and Hashknife wondered if he brought some liquor out to Buck.

Hashknife turned at the forks of the road and headed for Wolf Wells. He wanted to get away from the two ranches and mix with people. He felt that there was nothing to be learned from the people at either the Circle Cross or the Tomahawk; so why bother with them?

CHAPTER IX

IN THE Lily of the Valley saloon, Hashknife found Lonesome Hobbs and Bility Edwards. Lonesome's fat face was as placid as a mountain pool and his eyes were round and solemn. Bility was also very solemn of demeanor.

They both nodded to Hashknife, who invited them to partake of his hospitality. It was then that Hashknife discovered that Lonesome and Bility were gloriously, shamelessly drunk. Lonesome nearly fell down in merely turning around to the bar.

He looked at Hashknife, wide-eyed and said—

"Gotta roo—roosh-ter?"

"Got a rooster?"

"Yesh," nodded Bility, "Need one—bad."

"What for?" Hashknife grinned at their earnestness.

"Fight," explained Lonesome, trying to make the glass and bottle meet.

The bartender rescued them both, when Lonesome dropped them disgustedly.

"Whitey's got roosh'er," said Lonesome. "Pre'y good one, too, y'betcha. Fight'n rooshter. Yesshir, he's gone af'er it."

"Who's Whitey?" asked Hashknife.

"He owns the depot," said Bility with great deliberation.

Came the sound of unsteady footsteps, and Whitey Anderson bumped his way in through the front door. Anderson was in the same condition as Lonesome and Bility, and in his two hands he carried a bedraggled-looking rooster.

"C'mon with your fight'n animals," croaked Whitey. "Bring 'm big and bring 'm strong. H'rah, f'r my he-hen!"

"Misser Andershon," said Lonesome gravely, "shake han's with my ol' friend Hartley. Very ol' friend, 'ndeed."

"How doo-o-o," drawled Whitey, and let loose of his rooster to shake hands with Hashknife.

The frightened bird flipped to the top of the bar, volplaned across to the top of a pool-table and scooted out the back door, cackling wildly. Lonesome made a grab at it, but missed and fell flat on his face, while Bility stumbled across him and almost knocked the bar loose from its moorings.

But Whitey paid no attention to any one, except Hashknife.

"Yesshir, I'm glad t' meet ol' friend of Loneshome Hobbs. Whatcha shay your—"

He looked around and discovered Lonesome trying to get back to his feet.

"Shay, Loneshome, what shay friend's name? My gosh, you ain't got ap'plexy, have yuh? Face's all red."

"Who shoved me?" wailed Lonesome, feeling of his nose, which was bleeding slightly. "Who done it, I deman't' know immed'ly."

"You fellers go outside to do your bumpin'!" advised the barkeep angrily. "This ain't no corral."

"Where's m' rooshter?" demanded Whitey hotly, looking around. "Who's got 'm? Loneshome have you got'm?"

"Nug oomp guff," declared Lonesome, holding one hand tightly over his nose and mouth.

"He says he ain't got 'em," explained Bility solemnly.

"I think he's a liar, Whitey; let's shearch him."

Bility staggered into Lonesome and tried to feel in his pockets, but Lonesome protested strenuously and Hashknife had to pry them apart.

"Got'm in hish pocket," declared Bility.

"Can't be dood," Whitey shook his head violently. "Can't put rooshter in pocket."

"Tha's right!" exclaimed Bility. "Too wild. Let's shing a shong. What shay?"

"Not in here," declared the bartender. "You cowpunchers start to sing in here and I'll—"

"Don't go no further." Lonesome shook a warning finger at the bartender. "You've threated us s'ffidently, Misser Weed. We unnerstand yore at'tude perfec'ly; perfec'ly. You are not a frien' of a workin' man, so you ain't. I refuse to shing in yore housh. C'mon."

They strung out in single-file, with Hashknife bringing up the rear, and went into the street. Whitey leaned against the side of the building and tried to adjust his hat to an even balance.

"Mus' go back t' work," he declared, trying to force himself to a semblance of sobriety. "I'm workin' man."

"Ain't you goin't' shing?" queried Lonesome.

"Yesh, I'll shing—shometime—but not yet. Gotta work."

He shoved himself away from the wall and wended a very erratic way down the narrow sidewalk.

"Perfec'ly capable man," declared Lonesome airily, "but he's curshed with a thirsht. Ha, ha, ha! Rhymes like a po'm. Curshed with a thirsht."

"You think yo're funny, don'tcha?" queried Bility, with drunken sarcasm.

"Yesshir, I am. Betcha I c'n make you laugh."

"Zasso? Betcha five dollars yuh can't."

"Lissen, that's a bet, now."

Lonesome shook a finger in Bility's face.

"Can't back down, yuh mus' 'member."

"Nosshir, I back down from no man. How yuh goin' do it?"

"Take off yore boots, old shad face. I'm goin' to tickle yore feet."

"Tha's dirty trick," declared Bility. "That ain't bein' funny, you danged fathead—tha's torture. But I'll let yuh try it. I'm numb all over, anyway."

He half-fell to the edge of the sidewalk and began tugging at his boot, which resisted his efforts stubbornly. Lonesome essayed to help him and Hashknife walked away, leaving them in each other's arms and the boot still intact.

Hashknife crossed the street and bought some tobacco, after-which he sauntered down the street to the little depot. He found Whitey Anderson slumped in a chair, his head dripping wet and his shirt saturated.

"Water-cure," explained Whitey. "Dam near drowned myself, but it sure sobered me up. I get with that blamed gang up there and drink too much. Anyway—" Whitey hooked his toe into the rounds of a chair and jerked it around for Hashknife—"Anyway, I'm sick as of this town and this job. Nothin' ever happens, except somebody gets drunk and shoots up things a little. And I mostly always miss that."

"Wolf Wells seems like a nice town," observed Hashknife.

"It does? Well, you can have it, as far as I'm concerned. I'm goin' to have another station or I quit poundin' brass."

Hashknife laughed softly over his cigaret. "I should think you'd get lots of excitement. Train comin' in every day and all that."

"My God!" Whitey stared at Hashknife wonderingly.

"Trains comin' in—sa-a-ay, the only reason they ever come to Wolf Wells is because there's a Y here, and it makes the engineer seasick to ride backward. Never any passengers."

"One come in this mornin', didn't he?"

Whitey grew thoughtful for a moment.

"Uh-huh. That's right, we did have one today. Yessir, I remember that Carsten came in."

"Come very often?"

"Well, not every day," grinned Whitey. "He comes every month or so—him and his limp. Yuh know, a horse or a cow stepped on him about six month ago and busted his ankle."

"Cow or a horse?" grinned Hashknife. "Don't he know which it was?"

Whitey chuckled softly and helped himself to Hashknife's cigaret makings.

"I don't think he knows. Yuh see, it was in the dark. They was loadin' a train of stock out at the loadin'-corrals and Carsten was helpin'. He sure hollered to beat all. It kinda crippled him for a while."

"Does he buy a lot of stock around here?"

"Yeah, I think he does—quite a little. Mostly from the Circle Cross, though."

"That's what cuts down the profits on cattle—the freight," observed Hashknife. "By the time yuh pay for a lot of cars from here to Chicago, yuh ain't got much left."

"They don't pay the freight," explained Whitey. "The buyer pays 'em so much F. O. B. They've got to load 'em, of course. But I guess they get a pretty good price, at that."

"Are most of the cattle shipped, from here?"

"No-o-o. Mostly everythin' north of here ship from here, and the Flying M and the Circle Cross ship quite a lot, but the last two Circle Cross shipments went from the siding at Sandy, about five or six miles below here.

"That siding was put in for the 66 outfit, so they tell me; but any-body can use it. It's about as close to the Circle Cross as this is, and if they pick their cattle from the south range, it's closer."

"No town there?" queried Hashknife.

"Nope; not even a shed. Just a loading-corral, that's all."

A man came in to argue about an overdue express package, so Hashknife sauntered back uptown; He stopped to speak, with the sheriff, who was filled with gloom over the fact that his deputy was hors do combat.

"Lonesome's just plain drunk," he announced. "He's bad enough when he's sober. I found him and Edwards out in the street, with their boots off, tickling each other's feet. That's a hell of a thing for grown men to do."

Hashknife grinned widely and went back to his horse. He had tied the Sharps rifle to the horn of his saddle and now he rode away with it swinging in his hand. Instead of keeping to the road he turned into the hills and rode straight toward the Tomahawk.

* * * *

It was a broken country and he was forced to travel slowly, but it was much safer than to take chances of being shot at on the road. He passed the spot where he had picked up Poco's trail that morning, and swung wide around the coulée to come down at the west side of the Tomahawk. He had no wish to take a chance on being shot at again, although he did not expect the bushwhacker to be on the job again that day.

He came out on the brow of the hill and drew rein. There was no one in sight at the ranch-house. The sun was low over the Western hills and the air was filled with the lazy drone of insects. From down in the hills a cow bawled softly.

Suddenly the drowsy gray bronco threw up its head, ears for-ward, as it glanced almost at right angles, and to the east. Hashknife turned quickly and looked in that direction.

About four hundred yards away, a man was crossing the ridge; a man who stooped low in the sage and appeared to be carrying a rifle. He stopped and appeared to turn in their direction.

Hashknife knew that the man had seen him; so he whirled his horse around and spurred him into deeper cover. As Hashknife drew up he saw the man running in the opposite direction, still running crouched over, and disappeared over the ridge.

Hashknife debated quickly. This man was armed with a rifle, and if it was the bushwhacker, he knew how to use it. He had a decided advantage, over Hashknife, because he could stop just beyond the ridge and wait for Hashknife to come to him.

"He must 'a' been just givin' it up as a bad job," decided Hashknife, "and I caught him pullin' out. C'mon, bronc."

Hashknife rode back in the direction of the Tomahawk, but as soon as he crossed the top of the ridge, he spurred his horse into a gallop and cut the side of the hill toward where the man had disappeared. This left another ridge between where Hashknife rode and where the man had disappeared, and Hashknife felt sure that the man would not dare to try and cross back to his original position on the slope to the Tomahawk.

Hashknife rode about eight hundred yards along the side of the hill, swung back near the top and dismounted, leaving his horse in a heavy clump of grease wood. Cautiously he went to the top of the ridge and studied every inch of the country.

To the right of him was the spot where the man had crossed the next ridge, and Hashknife could see that the man had gone into a heavily wooded coulée. Minute after minute passed, but still Hashknife's eyes studied every bit of brush in sight.

But there was nothing, except the heat-haze of late afternoon. Across the coulée in a jumble of rocks a ground-hog whistled shrilly, angrily, as the shadow of a circling hawk passed over the rocks.

Hashknife grinned and reached for his tobacco.

"Everybody's gunnin' for somethin'," he said softly, "but a man is the weakest of all, when it comes to knowin' when to duck. The ground-hog knows what to dodge, and that hawk ain't got a chance to collect a feed. I suppose I'd know how to dodge bullets, if my ancestors for several hundred years back had been dodgin' 'em a few times per day all their lives."

Suddenly he caught sight of a moving object far down the coulée to his left. It was almost half a mile away, but he was able to see that it was a man on a pinto horse. As Hashknife watched him he swung to the right, climbed up a narrow coulée to the top of the ridge, where he stood, silhouetted against the sky, for several moments. Then he rode over the ridge and out of sight.

"Man on a pinto," mused Hashknife. "Too far away for a shot with this old gun, and, anyway, I don't know that he's the man I'm after."

He watched for about five minutes longer and went back to his horse, where he mounted and rode to the Tomahawk ranch-house.

They were all glad to see him, especially Sleepy, who was propped up in a chair, trying to teach Lorna to roll cigarets for him. Jimmy, the half-breed, was there but, like his aboriginal ancestors, did not ask questions.

Hashknife explained to Sleepy what had happened to him after leaving there that morning; told him of following Poco Saunders, and of seeing the man on the pinto.

"Jimmy," Hashknife turned to the half-breed, "who rides a pinto horse?"

Jimmy squinted thoughtfully and shook his head.

"Nobody, I guess. I have pinto long time ago, but him stole, I think."

"Long time ago? How long is a long time, Jimmy?"

"T'ree, four month, I think."

Lorna had been an interested listener, but now she exclaimed:

"Why, the man that shot Sleepy was riding a pinto! I did not think to tell you before."

"Pinto, pinto, who owns the pinto," laughed Hashknife. "There's no pinto on the Circle Cross. Buck Avery rides a Roman-nosed buckskin and a jug-headed roan. Poco has a sorrel and a bay; Trainor keeps four others at the stable, but there ain't a pinto in the outfit."

"Well," grinned Sleepy, "mother says I'll be ridin' in a day or so; and we'll find out who forks a painted bronc. You need me and my brains, cowboy."

"Uh-huh," Hashknife grinned widely. "I sure need yuh, Sleepy."

Lorna and her mother went into the kitchen and Sleepy motioned Hashknife to come closer.

"I'll tell yuh why Cassidy drew the deadline with the Circle Cross. It was because Trainor came to see Lorna and made love to her. He got drunk and bragged about it in Wolf Wells, it seems, and when Cassidy asked him if he was goin' to marry her—well, I reckon Trainor wasn't.

"Lorna didn't tell me, but her mother did. Smoky Cole came to see her a few times, too; but Mrs. Cassidy says that Smoky was nice boy."

Hashknife nodded slowly and looked straight at Sleepy.

"You ain't stuck on her, are yuh, Sleepy?"

Sleepy rubbed his hand thoughtfully on his knee, avoiding Hashknife's eyes for a moment, but looked up and said:

"No. She's goin' to marry Ben Lanpher, if he gets loose. They've been mighty good to me here, Hashknife. The old lady is a dinger, y'betcha. My own mother couldn't 'a' done more for me than she has. If old Cassidy don't get acquitted, I'm goin' down and blow a corner off that jail. Gotta do somethin' to show my appreciation."

Hashknife stayed to supper and spent the evening with them. Bright moonlight flooded the land when he started back for the Circle Cross, so he headed into the hills in preference to taking a chance along the lighted road. There were too many narrow places where a man might lie in wait with a sawed-off shotgun.

He rode slowly along the moonlit ridges, through the misty-gray-blue hills; silent, except for the occasional yipping bark of a coyote or the sleepy bawl of a cow. From far away came the faint whistle of a locomotive as the train drew near Wolf Wells.

Hashknife stopped his horse and rolled a cigaret. He could think clearer with a cigaret between his lips. He had the glimmering of an idea—a solution to the whole problem—but there were many tangles to straighten out, many loose ends to pick up yet.

"Gawd A'mighty," he said half-aloud. "I ain't askin' nothin' for me and Sleepy. That other two thousand that Lanpher offers us ain't worth prayin' for, but if you can see yore way clear to keep them dirty pups from fillin' us with lead until T can clean up this layout, I sure wish you'd do it. Amen. C'mon, bronc."

Which was the nearest thing to a prayer that Hashknife Hartley had ever offered—and it was not for himself or his partner—but for those who would profit more than gold.

* * * *

The trial of Ben Lanpher for the murder of Smoky Cole was the first case on the docket and caused much speculation in the Ghost Hills Range. They came from far and wide to sit in a hot, stuffy court-room and listen to the bickerings of the attorneys. Mitchell, the San Francisco lawyer, had worked swiftly in building up a defense, which he knew to be weak and insufficient. His only argument would be that Ben was too drunk to have done the deed.

There was no one who could say what kind of a bullet had killed Smoky Cole. Lanpher had told Mitchell about the doings of the bush-whacking rustlers, but Mitchell knew that there was little hopes of throwing the guilt upon a party or parties unknown; especially after Ben's hat and gun had been found near the murdered man.

The fact that Ben and Smoky had tried to shoot each other in town, and that Ben had left town ahead of Smoky, tended to weaken the defense badly.

Eph Baker, the prosecuting attorney, chewed tobacco and grinned benevolently upon everybody. Eph was fat, and the hot weather both-ered him considerably, but he realized that little effort would be nec-essary to win this case. He had prepared a scathing denunciation of young men who come to cowland and mix their whisky with six-guns.

It had cost him much in perspiration to prepare this tirade, but the heart within him rejoiced that he would be directing his verbal broad-sides at "city-folk" and not at the people of the range country. He felt sorry for the Lanpher family, and especially for the young lady, but Eph was cognizant of his place in the sun and was going to make a name for himself, in spite of his feelings.

Ben was a greatly changed young man since his few days in jail. He realized what his escapades had done for him and there was little doubt of his sincere repentance. His mother, sister and father sat at the table with Mitchell, while just away from them sat Ben and the sheriff.

Sleepy was able to sit in a saddle again and rode in with the fam-ily from the Tomahawk. He was a little pale and had not regained his full strength, but his six-gun swung at his hip and he prayed for an open shot at the man who had shot him from ambush.

The sheriff had questioned Hashknife regarding Lorna's identi-fication of the man, but Hashknife had evaded the question. Several other men, who had been at that meeting, tried to find out who she had meant, but Hashknife told nobody, except Trainor. The night after he had left the Tomahawk he had met Trainor at the front of the ranch-house and had told him what Lorna had said.

Trainor was very grave over the information, and tried to remember some one who might look or ride like Buck Avery, but was unable to do so. There seemed no doubt in his mind that Lorna was mistaken in the man, because of Buck's condition.

They both agreed to say nothing more about it. Buck's spree was over and he became a normal being once more. But Poco Saunders did not seem to relax for a moment. Hashknife felt that Poco was keying himself up to a point where he was going to kill somebody. Somehow, Hashknife felt that Poco knew the guilty man—or thought he did—but was waiting until he was sure.

And Hashknife had not been shot at for a day and a half, which showed that the Fantom Riders, whoever they might be, had relaxed their aggressiveness, or decided that he was a hard target to hit. Hashknife was inclined to favor the former.

The first day of the trial was devoted to securing a jury. Few challenges were used by either side, and the usual question—

"Have you formed any opinion as to the guilt or innocence of the defendant?" was omitted.

Every one conceded that it would be a short trial, because of there being no witnesses, except those who had seen Ben Lanpher ride away ahead of Smoky Cole. The old prospector had disappeared into the hills and no one knew where he had gone. No one knew where he had come from or who he was, and it was whispered that he might be one of the rustling gang.

Hashknife rode home that evening with Trainor and Buck, while Sleepy went back with the Cassidy family and Jimmy. The Lanphers had taken rooms at the hotel, intending to stay there during the trial. Poco remained in town, and Hashknife noticed that he was drinking a little.

Trainor and Hashknife discussed the case on the way home, but Buck had little to say.

"We've got to pull for Ben, thasall," observed Trainor. "He's up against a hard deal and I don't look for him to get loose."

"If he gets loose, Cassidy won't have much trouble," observed Hashknife. "Mitchell is goin' to work from the angle that there was bushwhackin' done before Smoky was killed and afterward. Mebbe he can convince that jury that Ben had no hand in it at all."

"He might," agreed Trainor.

Later on, Hashknife asked Buck what had become of Carsten and Buck told him that Carsten had stayed in town to see old man Shappee, but might be out to the Circle Cross the next day. Buck was not very communicative, so Hashknife let him alone. It was later in the evening that Poco came. He had been drinking, but the liquor only served to make him more quiet. Hashknife was outside the barn when Poco came out and they stood together for a while without speaking.

"Poco," said Hashknife seriously, "did you see the color of the horse you trailed?"

"Color?" Poco studied the question for a while, before he nodded and said—

"Yeah—a pinto."

"Who rides a pinto?"

"I've been tryin' to find out," said Poco slowly.

Quong's supper triangle stopped the conversation, and the trial was not discussed at the meal. Trainor seemed greatly preoccupied, Buck a little sullen and Poco quiet as usual.

Toward the end of the meal, Hashknife turned to Trainor.

"Why do they call this gang 'The Fantom Riders?'"

Trainor laughed shortly.

"I suppose it's because they work like ghosts, Hartley. Nobody has ever seen 'em."

"Has anybody ever tried to find 'em?"

Trainor leaned his elbows on the table and rested his chin on his hands.

"Tried to find 'em?" he repeated slowly, and laughed. "They sure have."

"There ain't much brains in the Ghost Hills, then," observed Hashknife slowly.

"What do you mean?" queried Trainor quickly, while Buck and Poco grew interested. Hashknife grinned and pursed his lips.

"Just what I said," he declared, squinting his eyes away from the smoke of his cigaret.

"It takes brains to catch ghosts."

"Mebbe you could catch 'em." Buck's remark was sarcastic, but Hashknife merely laughed at him.

"Sure I could catch 'em—if it was worth my while."

Trainor laughed and shook his head.

"I'm afraid they'd get you first, Hartley."

"Thasso? They've sure done enough shootin' at me. What I don't understand is how they ever hit anybody. Such poor shootin' as they've been doin'.'"

Hashknife knew that the marksmanship had been good enough, but the shooter had picked his targets at long range. Buck laughed shortly and got to his feet.

"Well," he said, "why don't yuh go out and get 'em? It'll be worth yore while, I reckon. The ranchers would be willin' to pay yuh well."

"Go ahead," grinned Trainor. "The Circle Cross will sure pay yuh a good reward and the others will chip in."

"By golly, I might, at that," laughed Hashknife.

"Lemme know when yuh start in," laughed Buck, "and I'll pick out a soft spot to bury yuh in, Hartley."

They finished their supper and went outside. It was growing dark and a slight breeze was blowing in from the north. A lone rider swung in through the main gate and rode up to them. It was Jimmy, the half-breed, and he spoke directly to Hashknife.

"You come."

"What's wrong now?" asked Hashknife quickly, thinking that the bushwhackers had been busy again.

"You come," repeated Jimmy and refused to say more.

Hashknife went straight to the barn and saddled his gray horse. Trainor came down and offered to go with him, but Hashknife shook his head.

"I'll find out what he wants, Trainor. Let yuh know later."

They rode away with the three men watching after them, and went straight down the road. Jimmy did not speak until they were past the forks and heading toward Wolf Wells. Then he swung off the road to the right and said—

"We go here."

It was just a little below where Hashknife had trailed Poco. There was no sign of a trail, but Jimmy went steadily on and into a brushy coulée where willows and cottonwoods grew in profusion. A tiny stream trickled over the rocks and on both sides the walls were almost precipitous. It was not a spot that a rider would choose in cutting across the country. The branches whipped Hashknife across the face in spite of their slow and cautious pace.

Suddenly Jimmy stopped and Hashknife rode in beside him. They were up against a brush corral. They dismounted and Jimmy led the way around to where three poles had been placed across the opening.

And just in front of them, plainly visible even in that weak light, stood a pinto horse. Hashknife studied the horse for a few moments and turned to Jimmy.

"Is that your pinto?"

"Mine," nodded Jimmy, "Tomahawk on left shoulder."

"How did yuh find him, Jimmy?" Hashknife could not keep the elation out of his voice, and he placed a hand on the half-breed's shoulder.

"I come through hills from town," explained Jimmy. "Down there," pointing back toward the road, "I find horse tracks. Rain make soft ground. Track point this way. I find 'nother horse track point this way.

"I wonder why horse come in this cañon. That's how I find. I come to you first. That my pinto, you bet."

"Good boy!" applauded Hashknife softly. "You're the smartest man in the Ghost Hills, Jimmy."

"Damn smart," admitted Jimmy proudly. "Now I take my pinto."

"Not yet," said Hashknife. "We've got to leave him here for a while, pardner. We know where he is, but we don't want anybody else to know that we know it; sabe?"

"Damn right!" exclaimed Jimmy. "I'm smart."

"Well," grinned Hashknife, "if we're both smart, we'd better get out of here right now. C'mon."

They went back to their horses, mounted and rode out of the cañon. Jimmy headed for the road, but Hashknife called him back and advised that they travel through the hills to the Tomahawk.

"Remember, they might be layin' for us," warned Hashknife. "We've got to be smart—me and you, Jimmy."

"You bet," agreed Jimmy. "I'm smart. Sometime damn fool. Jus' alike—mos' always."

"And you said a lot of wise words," laughed Hashknife.

They rode to the Tomahawk and Hashknife told Sleepy what they had found. Sleepy grinned with delight and fairly hugged Jimmy, the half-breed.

"But," said Hashknife sadly, "if that son-of-a-gun is as smart as he seems to be, he'll spot our horse-tracks. Yuh can't get into that place without leavin' plenty of sign."

"Well, what'll we do?" asked Sleepy.

"Be Johnny at the rat-hole," grinned Hashknife. "We've got to be there when he finds the tracks, Sleepy. We'll pull out of here before daylight and kinda drape ourselves on the edge of that cañon.

"We'll take that old Sharps along, and I'll bet he'll stop foolin' folks. You feelin' well enough for rough work, or do yuh reckon yuh better stay here and keep warm?"

"You try to stop me!" snapped Sleepy angrily.

"Pretty damn well," stated the old squaw. "Good man—git well quick."

Sleepy took several naps during the night, but Hashknife huddled in a chair and smoked innumerable cigarets. The discovery of the hidden horse had simplified things to a great extent. It meant that the bushwhackers had stolen the pinto and were using him for their work, instead of using their own horses, which might be easy of identification.

All night long Hashknife puzzled over different things, trying to untangle, a web of suspicions and bring them to a point where he could work upon a reasonable basis. There was nothing definite upon which to rest his suspicions, but he had the glimmering of an idea that might, if things worked out right, bring results.

CHAPTER X

HE WOKE Sleepy about two hours before daylight and they rode into the hills. To satisfy their own curiosity that the pinto had not been removed they went to the brush corral and looked at the animal.

Then they went back to the side of the cañon, hid their horses and sat down to wait. Daylight came, but nothing else. At nine o'clock they were both tired of the vigil. Both of them were to appear at the trial, and they felt that the pinto would not be moved that day, so they mounted and rode through the hills to Wolf Wells.

Train or, Carsten and Lanpher were together in the Antelope saloon when Hashknife and Sleepy arrived. Trainor invited them to have a drink, and afterward he and Carsten drifted away together.

Lanpher was frankly worried about the trial, although he tried to appear unconcerned. Hashknife drew him aside and they sat down together at a vacant card-table.

"I want to ask yuh a few questions," said Hashknife easily. "You handle the business end of the Circle Cross, don't yuh?"

"Yes," nodded Lanpher, "I handle most of it."

"How many head of cattle have you lost?"

Lanpher grimaced bitterly and shook his head.

"I don't know exactly, Hartley. The last roundup showed a big loss. I have talked with several other owners and they have lost more or less, but I think that we have been hit harder than any of them. Of course, we were the largest owners."

"You ought to be able to make a good guess at what you've lost," observed Hashknife. "You'd get a pretty fair count at the roundup, and you know how much you've sold."

Lanpher drew out a note-book and pencil, and, after making a few notes, tore out the page and handed it to Hashknife.

"There is the sales for this year, Hartley. I'll get the approximate roundup count from Trainor and give it to you later. He will know exactly what we started with, and what the average increase would be.

"I have never attended to that end of the thing because I have been too busy with my other interests. I am not a practical cattleman, but Trainor knows every phase of the business, and will be able to furnish you with facts."

Hashknife glanced at the notes and put the paper in his pocket

"I've got to check up on the amounts, or the approximate amounts of stolen stock, so as to get some idea of the bulk these thieves had to handle," he told Lanpher.

"Good idea," nodded Lanpher indifferently, as he got to his feet. "Court is about to open, I think."

He walked away toward the court room, and Hashknife sauntered down the street to the depot. Whitey Anderson was tilted back in an old chair, his feet on the table and a cob-pipe between his teeth.

"Howdy," he greeted Hashknife. "Come in and rest your feet. How come you ain't at the trial?"

"Danged place is too stuffy," grinned Hashknife, seating himself on the counter beside the clattering telegraph instrument.

"I probably won't be called before afternoon, anyway."

Hashknife rolled a cigaret and listened to the clicking sounder, although he did not understand the difference between a dot and a dash.

"Say, I got into a kind of a mix-up over a darned telegram," he told Whitey. "Along about the tenth of this month I sent a telegram to a certain party here in Wolf Wells and he swears he never got it."

"Swears he didn't?"

Whitey twisted the pipe-stem between his teeth and looked foolishly solemn.

"Swears he didn't get it, eh?"

"Yeah," Hashknife nodded seriously. "I think the darned jughead got it all right, but didn't want to answer it. Telegrams don't get lost, do they, Whitey?"

"Hm-m-m! Might—but they don't very often. About the tenth, eh? Who was it sent to, Hartley?"

"Well, I don't want to say," laughed Hashknife, "but if I knowed for sure, I'd make him a little bet that he got it."

"By golly, I'd know if he got it."

Whitey got to his feet rather belligerently.

Hashknife laughed softly.

"Don't get mad, Whitey, but this feller said that you'd likely got drunk and lost it."

"Is that so!"

Whitey slammed his pipe down on the counter and drew a bulky, flimsy-leafed volume from under the counter-top. He began flipping over the leaves, grunting to himself, while Hashknife peered over his shoulders, scanning the imprint of the telegrams.

Page after page flipped past, until certain dates caused Whitey to scan them closer. Carefully they looked them over.

"Did yuh sign your own name?" asked Whitey, going back over certain dates carefully.

"Yeah, I sure did," said Hashknife, his eyes shining with sudden delight.

"Well—" Whitey slapped the book shut and tossed it back under the counter—

"Well, it never came to this office, Hartley—That's a cinch. Where did yuh send it from?"

"Phoenix," lied Hashknife. "Dang it, I thought this feller just didn't want to admit it, but I guess it got lost."

"Well, you can tell him that I didn't lose it," said Whitey half-angrily. "And you can tell him that I've only been drunk twice since I came here."

"Aw, don't mind him," laughed Hashknife. "He was drunk when he said it."

Hashknife wandered back uptown, sat down on the board sidewalk and scribbled a few words on the back of an old envelope. He seemed pleased with himself, as he softly sang:

> "I loved a maiden, whose hair was like go-o-old,
> And her eyes were as blue as the se-e-e-ea.
> She said she'd be tr-r-r-rue,
> But didn't say who to-o-o.
> I know now that she didn't mean me-e-e-e.
>
> Oh, I'm goin' to Montana,
> The trail's mighty long-g-g,
> But a trail's always shorter
> When I'm singin' my so-o-ong."

Hashknife wailed that last soft note and grinned at his own efforts. He was not musical. In fact, he hardly knew the difference between "Home, Sweet Home" and "Little Brown Jug," except for the difference in words.

And it was not often that Hashknife sang; but just now he felt that he was entitled to lift his voice in song. Trainor was coming up the sidewalk with old man Shappee and Hashknife joined them. They were going to a restaurant; so Hashknife went along.

"You won't have to be a witness," said Trainor, as they sat down. "The sheriff and Lonesome testified about findin' the body, and told about you bein' with them. It would only be a case of repeatin' the testimony."

"I don't reckon that the prisoner has got a chance in the world," declared Shappee. "I never seen such a weak defense as he's got. By God, I feel sorry for Lanpher; but I'd have to convict him, if I was on that jury."

"Looks bad for him," agreed Trainor. "It looks bad."

"Well, it's just so danged weak that the case will go to the jury in the mornin'," said Shappee. "It ain't what you'd call interestin'. Eph Baker's got a cinch case and he knows it."

"Well," grinned Hashknife, "yuh never can tell."

"No, that's a fact. Cow-country juries are funny things."

After lunch Trainor drew Hashknife aside and tried to find out why Jimmy, the half-breed, came after him; but Hashknife only laughed and told him that Sleepy had sent for him.

"Jimmy made it look like somethin' important," grinned Hashknife, "but it wasn't."

Trainor lifted his eyebrows slightly, as if in disbelief, but Hashknife said nothing more. Carsten limped up from the courtroom and announced his intentions of getting some food, and in a few minutes court adjourned and Sleepy joined Hashknife.

The Lanpher family came along together and Hashknife noticed that Mrs. Lanpher had been crying. He went to them and tried to laugh away their fears.

"There ain't nothin' as bad as it looks," he told her. "You keep on grinnin', ma'am."

"There seems to be little cause for smiles," said Helen wistfully. "Everything is wrong."

Hashknife shook his head quickly.

"No, m'am; that's the wrong way to think. Down deep in yore heart you know danged well that Ben didn't do it. He knows he didn't; but when he looks at yuh and sees yuh cryin' and looking goshawful sad—well, he kinda figures that yuh ain't with him.

"Cryin' is fine sometimes." Hashknife turned to Mrs. Lanpher, as though half-apologizing. "Yessir, it sure helps once in a while. But if you needed help real bad, would yuh expect to' get it from a cryin' person or one that smiles?"

"I can see your point," said Mrs. Lanpher sadly, but trying to smile.

"Certainly, we all can," said Lanpher.

Mrs. Cassidy, the squaw, Lorna and Jimmy were coming from the courtroom and the Lanphers moved aside to let them pass on the narrow sidewalk.

Lorna stopped and looked at Mrs. Lanpher.

"Why do you cry?" she asked softly. "Are you afraid?"

Mrs. Lanpher forced a smile as she shook her head.

"I am trying to not be afraid, child."

Lorna nodded and looked up at Hashknife.

"We are not afraid, are we?"

It was not what she said or the way she said it that made Hashknife stutter his reply of—

"Yuh—yuh bet we ain't, Lorna."

She smiled around at them and hurried to catch up with her mother, while the Lanphers looked after her.

"There's the prettiest girl in the world," declared Hashknife aloud, although he had meant to say it only to himself. Sleepy was looking queerly at him and Hashknife blushed hotly.

"Was Ben really going to marry her?" asked Helen.

"Is going to," corrected Sleepy.

"Not if I can prevent it;" declared Lanpher quickly.

"Which you can't," smiled Hashknife.

Trainor and Carsten joined them; so Hashknife and Sleepy walked down the street and crossed over to the Antelope saloon, where they found Poco and Buck Avery. Poco was drinking steadily, but the whisky showed little effect on him.

Several poker-games were in progress, and in a few minutes Carsten and Trainor came in and took seats in a game. Carsten spoke to Poco, but only received a black look for his courtesy. Poco was in no mood for companionship.

Hashknife and Sleepy stayed around town for an hour or so, but did not go to the courtroom. The place was crowded to the doors and the sun beat down on the old frame building with great intensity.

Poco watched them mount and ride back toward the ranch and in a few minutes he mounted and went out of town, sitting very straight in spite of all he had drunk during the day.

Hashknife and Sleepy went straight to the brush corral and found the pinto still there. It was evident that the Fantom Riders were not aware that their hidden mount had been discovered—or perhaps they did not care.

"Mebbe they've found out that we know about the pinto and will quit comin' here," suggested Sleepy.

"They might, but I don't believe it," said Hashknife. "Somethin' caused 'em to lay off us for a while; but they'll be back. They won't lay off us until they're behind the bars or we're under the grass."

"I'll choose the latter," said Sleepy seriously. "I've always wished to have 'Grand-paw' carved on my tombstone. But I s'pose I'll poke my nose into trouble along with you until somebody'll select me a tenor-harp, which won't match my sopranner voice a-tall."

Hashknife shook his head.

"No, I don't reckon we're born to be shot, Sleepy. We've been shot at with everythin' except a bow and arrows, ain't we?"

"And sling-shots," laughed Sleepy. "But some danged poor shot will nail us both with a .22 some of these days. That's fate, old-timer."

"Well, we ain't learnin' nothin' by settin' here," said Hashknife, getting to his feet: He looked down at the brush corral and scanned the gray hills, where the heat-haze danced in Waves.

"I'll tell yuh what to do, Sleepy. You go back to the Tomahawk and get a good sleep. Take it easy until an hour or so before daylight. Then you take that old Sharps rifle and come down here. Locate yourself where yuh can watch this pinto; sabe?"

"And if anybody comes after it, I'll shoot 'em loose from their disposition," nodded Sleepy eagerly.

"Make sure that it ain't me, cowboy."

"Well, I'll sure know the shape of his jaw before I pull the trigger of that old dreadnaught, y'betcha. What are you goin' to do, Hashknife?"

"I'm goin' to the Circle Cross for the night; but you'll sure see me or hear from me early in the mornin'. You better stick to the hills all the way home, Sleepy."

"Danged right. I've only got one life to give for my country, and I'm sure goin' to be stingy with that. Look out for yourself, long feller."

Hashknife watched Sleepy ride away up the brushy slope, and swung back across the swale at the bottom of the corral cañon. He rode slowly, skirting the side of the hill until he reached the other swale above the road, where he had trailed Poco Saunders.

Near the cottonwood clump he dismounted and looked closely at the ground. There were a number of horse-tracks, jumbled together; some hardly visible, which were made before the rain.

Hashknife studied them closely, leading his horse from place to place. Then he found the imprint of a high-heeled boot, where a man had dismounted.

"Now what did he get off for?" wondered Hashknife as he scanned the swale.

The clump of old cottonwoods attracted him, so he led his horse down toward them. Farther down he found another heel-print, pointing toward the trees.

He walked up to the clump dropped his reins and looked around. There was nothing visible. He entered the clump and studied it from all angles. The road was not visible from any point in there.

"They didn't hide here to bushwhack anybody, that's a cinch," he muttered. "Smoky was probably shot from the other side of the road, and Jimmy, the half-breed, was shot from that direction."

Hashknife rolled a cigaret and leaned against the bole of one of the trees. As he passed the paper across his lips he lifted his head and glanced into the foliage. For a moment he stared intently and the cigaret slipped from between his fingers.

Just about the height of a man's reach, hanging closely against the gray bark of the old cottonwood, was a rifle in a canvas and leather scabbard. It was so nearly the color of the old bark that it would hardly be visible, unless seen at close quarters.

Hashknife stepped over and unhooked the strap off the short limb. The rifle was a Winchester,. 30-30, wrapped in oiled cloth, and filled with cartridges. He examined it closely and noted the peep sights, the well-kept mechanism and the polished bore.

Then he took out his pocket-knife, opened the screw-driver blade and grinned widely as he deftly ruined the firing-pin. Then he wrapped the gun in its oiled-cloth, slid it back into the scabbard and replaced it as he had found it.

He went back to his horse, mounted and circled back a mile into the hills before striking the road and heading for the Circle Cross. And for the first time since coming to the Ghost Hills Range, he relaxed in his saddle and sang softly, all unconscious of his words or music!

> *"There's a range far away in a beautiful land,*
> *Where cowboys live happy and free-e-e;*
> *And all decks have six aces*
> *All the girls pretty faces,*
> *O-o-oh, that is the land for me-e-e-e.*
>
> *I'm goin' to Montana,*
> *The trail's mighty long-g-g,*
> *But a trail's always shorter.*
> *When I'm singin' my song."*

* * * *

Trainor came to the ranch alone that evening. He said that Buck had started drinking again and would probably stay in Wolf Wells that night. The case had gone to the jury that afternoon.

"You've got to give Eph Baker a lot of credit," said Trainor, as they sat down to supper.

"He didn't make any plea. He knows that the case is a dead open-and-shut; so he told the judge and jury that he would not make any plea. Mitchell had little to say.

"He talked kinda soft to the jury and asked them to remember that murder had been done from ambush twice just a short time before, and had been attempted since.

"He pointed out the fact that Ben was just a wild kid and was drunk at the time. No, Mitchell didn't have no defense to speak of."

"Then you think they'll hang the kid?" queried Hashknife.

"No-o-o; they'll likely send him up for life."

"Life's a long time," mused Hashknife, sadly. "Didja ever think what that means, Trainor? It don't even give yuh a fightin' chance. Day after day, day after day—knowin' that yuh can't ever get out."

"Feller had better die fightin'," nodded Trainor.

"Yeah, that would be better. But what's after death? Do we go into a better world, I wonder. I often wonder if cows and horses live in the hereafter."

"That's a hell of a thing to think about," grunted Trainor. "Man would go loco tryin' to think about it. My theory is this: When yore dead, yore dead—and that's all there is to it."

"Then what's the use of livin' and tryin' to make somethin' of yourself, Trainor? What good does it all do yuh? Nossir, I think that there's somethin' else."

"Why should there be?" growled Trainor.

"Because God had somethin' in mind when he created man. He gave men and women a soul—or whatever it is that makes us what we are. Where does that go when the body dies. Does it die, too. You believe in God, don't yuh, Trainor?"

Trainor shoved away his plate and bit off the end of a cigar before he said:

"I've never had time to believe in anythin' that I can't see. Whatcha tryin' to do, start a revival?"

"Only what yuh can see?" laughed Hashknife. "Then yuh don't believe you've got a heart inside yuh, eh?"

"Damn, I can feel that!"

"Some folks claim they can feel God A'mighty."

"Aw-w-w hell!"

Trainor kicked back his chair and strode into the living-room, while Hashknife grinned at Quong and held out his cup for more coffee.

Quong grinned and shuffled over with the pot

"I no sabe Melican God," he said softly. "I sabe Chinese God, you bet. Plenty good."

"They're all the same, Quong. Do right all the time, help everybody, sing and smile. That's God, Quong."

"You damn right! You be plenty bad, you catch hell sure."

"And yuh don't have to die to get it either."

"Nossah. Plenty catchum lite here."

Hashknife grinned and followed Trainor into the living room, where he found the Circle Cross owner humped over in a rocking-chair, reading a newspaper. He grunted at Hashknife, but did not look up.

"When does the sheriff start his posse combin' the hills?" asked Hashknife.

Trainor glanced up at him, but turned back to his paper.

"How do I know?" he growled.

"I just wondered."

Hashknife walked to the front door and squinted off across the hills. He leaned against the doorway and looked back at Trainor.

"Say, I'll betcha he don't never do it. Trainor."

"Eh?"

Trainor turned his head quickly.

"Why won't he?"

Hashknife laughed shortly, seriously.

"Trainor, I've come to the conclusion that the best thing I can do is to plumb ruin these Fantom Riders."

"Yeah?"

Trainor placed his newspaper on the table and swung his chair around. Hashknife's statement was worth his undivided attention, but the half-grin on his lips showed that he was a trifle skeptical.

"Just how do you intend to do this, Hartley?" he asked.

"By exposing the Fantom Riders."

Trainor squinted closely at Hashknife, as if trying to see if he was joking; but the tall cowboy's face was very serious.

"Yeah?" Trainor laughed shortly. "Well, just how are you goin' to do that?"

"I ain't quite sure," Hashknife grinned thoughtfully and shook his head. "I've got the goods on 'em right now, but I don't want to tell anybody until I get set."

"Got the goods on 'em, eh? Tell me a little about it."

"Nope. I ain't just sure enough yet, but I'll make yuh a little bet that by this time tomorrow everybody'll know who's been doin' all the stealin' and shootin' around here."

"That's worth a bet," smiled Trainor, "but the odds are all against yuh, Hartley."

"I'll bet even money," said Hashknife firmly. "I've got five hundred dollars that says I'm right. If you want to cover that amount—go ahead."

Trainor laughed and shook his head.

"Not until I know more than I do now. You seem to think you have a cinch, and I never bet against a cinch."

"No, it ain't a cinch, Trainor. I think I know who has been doin' the shootin'; and the man or men who have been doin' the shootin' are the same ones that have been doin' the rustlin'. Tomorrow mornin' I'm goin' to ask a few questions in Wolf Wells, and what I learn will either cinch the case against 'em or bust my theory entirely."

"Well—" Trainor turned back to the newspaper—"I wish yuh luck, Hartley."

"Thank yuh," said Hashknife and clumped down the steps, going to the bunk-house.

For a long time he sat on his bunk in the dark bunk-house, humped over with his elbows on his knees, thinking of what he was going to do. Piece by piece he knitted the elusive evidence together; his lean jaws shut tightly, as he debated just what to do.

In all the years that he and Sleepy had untangled range mysteries and troubles, this was the most fiendish outfit they had ever tried to run to earth. The cattle stealing end of the thing was on a par with any rustling trouble, except the clever way in which it had been done; but the fact that three men had died from ambush; shot from behind, without a chance to protect themselves, while others had almost lost their lives, made it entirely different from anything they had ever encountered.

"They don't deserve a trial," muttered Hashknife. "Killin' ain't bad enough. I can forgive a rustler, but I can't stand for a dirty murderer."

Neither Buck nor Poco showed up that night, which was not surprizing, and Trainor rode away fairly early, after asking Hashknife if he was going to town with him.

Hashknife was in no hurry. He cleaned his six-shooter carefully, put on a clean shirt after shaving and took his time about saddling his horse. Then he rode away unhurried. At the forks of the road he turned toward the right, as if heading for the Tomahawk, spurring his gray into a gallop.

But as soon as he galloped around the first curve he reined off the road and pointed into the hills, circling toward where he had found the hidden rifle. Here he was forced to slow down to a walk on account of the rough going.

It was an ideal morning. The early morning mists were still rising up the sides of the gray hills; a meadow-lark warbled from the cottonwoods, and a flock of turtledoves, like fast-moving shadows, hurtled past on their way to a water-hole.

The gray horse threw up its head in alarm when a long-legged jack-rabbit bounded from under a sagebush, jigged a few times to loosen up its kinks and faded away into the protective coloring.

But Hashknife was not considering the beauties of nature just then. He rode very straight in his saddle, his six-shooter swinging loose in his right hand, while his eyes searched every movement on the brush-lined hills.

He was nearing the clump of trees in the little swale now, and the gray had slowed down to a slow walk. Once he drew up and made a motion, as if to dismount, but did not.

Suddenly a shot crashed out. The gray jerked back and Hashknife instinctively ducked. There was a brushy ridge between him and the shooter. For a moment Hashknife thought the shot had been fired at him, but the next moment came the spattering reports, as two guns opened a rapid fire.

Hashknife's first thought was that Sleepy had engaged the enemy. Forgetful of all danger to himself he spurred the gray into a lunging run and swept over the ridge and into the swale, circling wide above the clump of trees.

The tall gray hurdled sage and grease-wood, like a born hunter. Suddenly a horse came sweeping into them, its rider crouched low. Both horses were running at full speed, crossing each other at almost right-angles.

Two six-guns spat bullets at almost the same moment, and Hashknife felt the hot sear of a bullet across the side of his neck. A swift sidewise glance showed the other rider sway in the saddle, but the next instant horse and rider swept out of sight.

Hashknife tried to stop his lunging mount, but only managed to stop it almost against the grove of cottonwoods. He whirled in his saddle and tried to catch a glimpse of the other rider, but in vain. The gray hills had swallowed him up.

A moment before, two wild riders had almost crashed into each other; both had fired with the intent to kill. Now a meadow-lark winged its way into the quiet swale and lifted its voice in song.

Hashknife felt tenderly of his neck and got stiffly out of his saddle. Lying just a few feet away was the .30-30 rifle and around it was scattered four unexploded cartridges.

Hashknife smiled grimly and climbed back into his saddle, leaving the gun where he found it He jerked out the empty shell from his gun and replaced it with a fresh one.

Then he spurred into a gallop again and went straight for the spot where he had told Sleepy to meet him. And the faithful Sleepy was right there, fairly bursting to know the meaning of those shots.

"Damn it, I stayed here," he wailed. "I'm never where there's anythin' goin' on. What and who was it, Hashknife?"

"Get on yore bronc and come on," ordered Hashknife and Sleepy lost no time in following orders.

They spurred down out of the hills and headed for town before Hashknife yelled back at him:

"Shake up yore old coyote-bait, cowboy. I just swapped lead with Poco Saunders and I want to beat him to Wolf Wells."

"Poco Saunders!" yelled Sleepy. "Didja hit him?"

"I hope not I swapped before I thought."

"Hope not?" panted Sleepy, trying to urge his horse to greater speed in hopes of keeping up with the racing gray. "Why in hell do yuh hope not, Hashknife?"

"I'll tell yuh in town," yelled back the lanky one.

CHAPTER XI

TRAINOR met the Lanpher family at the hotel. Carsten was with them, and they were anxiously waiting for news of the jury which had been locked up all night, battling out the fate of Ben Lanpher.

Many of the ranchers and cowboys were still in town, anxious to know the verdict, and the Lily of the Valley and the Antelope saloons had profited greatly thereby.

There was an air of utter despair about the Lanpher family. They realized that nothing short of a miracle could save Ben from paying the extreme penalty for the crime.

The fact that the jury was still battling for a verdict showed that some of the members were unconvinced one way or the other. Lanpher paced the short lobby of the little hotel, his lips twitching nervously, paying no attention to the words of comfort from Carsten and Trainor.

Mrs. Lanpher and Helen sat together, staring out of the dusty window, seemingly resigned to their fate, speaking to no one. Mrs. Cassidy, the squaw, and Lorna had stayed at the hotel, awaiting the verdict, and now they came down the narrow stairway, scanning the faces of the group, as though wondering what the morning was to bring.

Trainor spoke to Lorna, but she did not look at him. After a glance around the room she went straight to Mrs. Lanpher and Helen, who looked up at her.

"You worry too much," said Lorna softly, and then, as though imparting a great truth:

"Sleepy says to not worry. Everything come out right pretty soon."

Trainor and Carsten moved in closer.

"Who is Sleepy?" queried Mrs. Lanpher.

"Oh, just a cowpuncher," said Trainor. "He is a friend of Hartley, who works for us, Mrs. Lanpher."

"Just a cowboy?" Lorna spoke softly and looked straight at Trainor.

"That's all he is," Trainor seemed slightly angry, and turned away, as if to dismiss the argument.

Lorna turned to Mrs. Lanpher.

"I don't know why he says that everything will come out right. He says—" Lorna smiled softly—"that you'll always have good luck when you find a pinto horse."

"Pinto horse?" asked Lanpher, ceasing his restless pacing of the floor. "What about a pinto?"

Trainor and Carsten were looking at Lorna, but she did not turn away from Mrs. Lanpher.

"I do not understand," said Mrs. Lanpher. "How can a pinto horse bring one good luck?"

Lorna shook her head seriously.

"I don't know, Mrs. Lanpher."

Trainor laughed sarcastically.

"Indian superstition, Mrs. Lanpher," he assured her.

"That damn lie!" grunted Mrs. Cassidy blandly, and Trainor's face went black with rage at the retort.

"Well," Lanpher laughed shortly, "Mrs. Cassidy should be a judge of that, Trainor. Personally, I hope that a pinto is good luck. There doesn't seem to be much luck for us here."

Trainor bit savagely at his underlip and strode out of the door, with Carsten going out behind him. They crossed to the Antelope and disappeared. Mitchell, the lawyer, came in and sat down.

"Nothing from the jury-room," he said wearily. "They seem to be at odds over something. They are a hard-headed lot of cattle-men, and I feel that we shall get the benefit of any doubt. Still, our defense was so weak; so weak that the prosecution was content to send the case to a jury on our own evidence and plea."

Lanpher blinked painfully and walked to the door. Mrs. Lanpher was crying softly and Mrs. Cassidy was looking at her, with a face as immobile as bronze. Then she said:

"You lose boy—you cry. Mebbe I lose husban'—I no cry. Too damn much cry; not 'nough laugh."

Lanpher had been leaning out, looking down the street, and now he turned back to those inside the lobby.

"The jury has reached a verdict," he half-whispered, and there was a decided catch in his voice, as he added—

"We—we'll know it all very soon."

Lonesome Hobbs came puffing up to the door and nodded violently.

"They—they've agreed," he panted. "I—I guess they gug-got hungry."

He turned and bow-legged his way across the street to notify every one, while those in the hotel lobby went slowly down to the courtroom; anxious, but still afraid to hear what the decision might be.

The courtroom filled rapidly. Trainor and Carsten took seats at the table with the Lanpher family, and in a few minutes the sheriff brought Ben in the rear door. Ben was pale and appeared nervous, jerky. He sat down beside the sheriff and stared straight at the wall, ignoring the sheriff's attempt at conversation.

The courtroom buzzed with subdued conversation which ceased quickly when the gray-haired judge came in and sat down at his desk. The judge appeared tired and worn as he looked down at the prisoner and scanned the room.

Then with a slow tread the jury filed in past the judge and sat down. Every eye in the room was upon them, and they seemed carefully to avoid looking at the prisoner who, after a searching glance, bowed his head.

The judge rapped softly for order, and turned to the jury.

"Gentlemen of the jury, have you reached a decision?"

Caleb Hardy, a raw-boned cattleman from the west side of the county, got slowly to his feet, holding a folded paper in his two big hands.

"Judge, we have," he said slowly, the lines of his face deepening, as he looked at the paper. "Yeah, we have. It's all wrote out on this here paper."

He stepped slowly across the intervening space and handed it to the judge. The room was so still that one might hear the buzzing of flies on the window-panes, as the judge unfolded the paper and read it. For a moment he looked at the rear of the room, his eyes half-closed. Then he looked down at Ben Lanpher and said softly—

"Ben Lanpher, stand up."

Ben glanced up at him for several moments before he got slowly to his feet, his hands resting on the table-top. The judge looked down at the paper and read aloud—

"We, the jury, find Ben Lanpher guilty of murder in the first degree."

The paper slid from his fingers and he shut his eyes, as if he did not want to see how Ben Lanpher took the blow.

Ben stared at him, turned his head and looked out across the silent crowd, his jaw set tight. Mrs. Lanpher began crying bitterly, and Ben stared at her, as if he did not understand what it was all about. Then he sat down and leaned forward on his folded arms, while the sheriff patted him on the back and tried to say words that would not come from his lips.

The judge turned to the jury.

"Gentlemen, is this your verdict?"

They nodded slowly, and the foreman said hoarsely—

"Judge, it was all we could do."

Trainor got up and crossed to Ben, offering his sympathy and hope; but Ben did not look up. Lanpher shoved Trainor aside and threw an arm around the boy's shoulder.

The room had been silent, as the audience watched every move of the main actors in the drama, but now there came the scrape of a footstep at the front door and Buck Avery came in. He started for the front of the room, but some one caught hold of him, whispering for him to be still.

But Buck struck the hand aside and started down the aisle, just as the rear door swung open and Hashknife and Sleepy came in. As intent as the audience was on the prisoner, they gave more than passing interest to these two cowboys, who had used the private entrance to get into the room.

Hashknife and Sleepy stopped near the judge's desk and looked over the room. Lorna and her mother looked at them and they both smiled. Buck had halted about midway of the room in the center aisle, as if undecided what to do.

"Ben Lanpher, stand up," said the judge hoarsely.

Ben did not hear him and the sheriff repeated the order. Ben stood up, his hand on his father's shoulder, and looked straight at the grave-faced old judge.

"Ben Lanpher, you have been found guilty of murder in the first degree, and it is the duty of this court to carry out that verdict. Is there any reason why I should not pronounce sentence upon you here and now?"

Ben looked away from the judge and down at his father.

"No," Ben shook his head. "I—I guess—not."

"There is a reason, judge."

Hashknife had spoken softly, but his voice carried to the far end of the room like a trumpet.

The judge turned and looked at him in amazement. Eph Baker, the prosecutor, was on his feet in a moment.

"I object to this!" he snapped. "What right—"

"There's a mighty good reason, judge," said Hashknife slowly, never taking his eyes off the crowd.

"If you'll let me, I'll tell yuh why. If yuh won't, I'll tell it anyway."

"I protest against this interference," insisted Baker, appealing to the judge, who was staring at the cowboys.

"Set down, you fat hoptoad," laughed Sleepy, and Baker's teeth snapped angrily.

"Well, it is irregular," hesitated the judge, "but—"

Mitchell was already on his feet and before the judge.

"Let him talk, your honor," he begged. "It is a God-sent interference, if they have evidence."

"Little bright-eyes over there is havin' a fit," said Sleepy, pointing at Eph Baker, who was struggling to swallow his anger.

Some one in the audience laughed cacklingly and a ripple of laughter followed. The Lanpher family were staring at Hashknife and Sleepy, as if afraid that something would interfere with their last-minute assistance.

"The court will listen," decided the judge, and there was evident relief in his voice.

"I'm sure much obliged," said Hashknife slowly. "We're sorry to be so late—but better late than never."

He cleared his throat and hooked his thumbs over his sagging belt, while Sleepy moved back until he was against the judge's desk.

"You've all heard about the Fantom Riders," said Hashknife, a half-grin on his lips.

There was a perceptible movement in the crowd, a shuffling of feet, the clink of a spurred heel.

"And you've all lost more or less stock," continued Hashknife. "It's been a mystery where them cows went to. The Circle Cross lost a lot of cows; so Mr. Lanpher decided to hire a cattle detective, and gave him work as a cowpuncher.

"The Fantom Riders killed him. They hired another. Pinto Cassidy is charged with his murder, because he was killed on the Tomahawk ranch. Yuh see," Hashknife grinned, "Pinto Cassidy drew a deadline between his ranch and the Circle Cross.

"Mr. Lanpher kinda run out of detectives. There wasn't much use, it seemed. The criminals got wise to 'em as soon as they showed up, and a feller ain't got much chance to stay in the game when men shoot from the brush.

"Me and my pardner—" Hashknife pointed at Sleepy—"We hired out to lay the ghosts. Nobody, except Lanpher, knew who we were. He hired us in San Francisco, and we sneaked in here without any brass bands. Not a danged soul knowed who we were—but they started shootin' at us right away."

Hashknife shifted his feet and his eyes narrowed a trifle. His smile was all gone now. Even Ben Lanpher had forgotten that he was a condemned murderer, and was watching and listening.

"They even mistook Jimmy, the half-breed, for me, and plugged him in the arm. They sure wasted a lot of lead and got little results. They plugged Sleepy once.

"I wondered how they spotted us so quick. I hired out to the Circle Cross, after Smoky Cole, the foreman, had been killed. Of course, Ben Lanpher was arrested for that killin'.

"I think I know why Smoky was killed, folks. Smoky was a hard drinker, a man who didn't want to be bossed, and he might—talk."

"Wait just a moment," interrupted Baker. "Is this all guess work on your part? If you have proven facts—"

"Set down!" growled Sleepy angrily. "You can ask some questions after he's all through."

Baker subsided reluctantly.

Hashknife laughed shortly and started to speak, but Sleepy interrupted with:

"Buck Avery, I wish you'd set down. Yuh make me nervous standin' there in the aisle."

Buck snarled back a short answer, which was not intelligible, and a man moved over for him to sit down, but Buck ignored him.

"Go ahead, Hashknif e; he won' t set down—yet," said Sleepy, and Hashknife continued:

"Until we came here, nobody had ever seen the Fantom Riders. We seen him—on a pinto horse; so we had that much evidence. But nobody around here, except Jimmy, the half-breed, owned a pinto; and Jimmy's pinto had been stolen.

"The shootin' had all been done with a .30-30 rifle; but they all shoot the same size ammunition, which made it hard to prove which .30-30 fired the shots. Are yuh all interested in my story?"

"Keep weavin', brother!" exclaimed a cowboy earnestly.

"Well, I got to wonderin' about that dead-line," said Hashknife thoughtfully.

"Men don't draw deadlines just for fun; so I went on a still-hunt for a reason—and found it. Pinto Cassidy is in jail for killin' that detective on Tomahawk property, but he never killed him. It was a damn easy thing to put that dead man there and lay the blame on the old man."

"Can you prove that?" asked Baker quickly.

"I can. But I reckon I'd better let yuh into the mystery of the stolen cattle. It started over a certain feller wantin' a girl. Her pa and ma didn't want her to marry him; so he decided to get even with pa and ma by bustin' up their herds.

"He got kinda stuck on another girl, but because she wasn't white, he wanted to love her, but not as a wife. It's things like that, gents, that causes dead-lines."

"What do you mean?" roared Trainor. "You mean to say that I—"

Hashknife ignored him, but Sleepy's eyes never left Trainor's face, as Hashknife continued:

"There was only one man who could have told that me and Sleepy were comin' here to work on this case. We met him in Lanpher's home in Frisco. He was the link to a weak chain of evidence. I needed him; so I got a look at a telegram down at the depot. Here it is."

Hashknife produced an old envelope and read aloud—

"Lanpher makes private shipment of one long one medium. 'Watch for them soon.'"

"That was the telegram I discovered, and I knowed it was the wire that caused us to be met with bullets. Then—" Hashknife shoved the letter into his pocket—"Then Jimmy stumbled on to the pinto. It was back in the hills in a brush corral, hidden away. The bushwhacker could switch horses there any old time. It sure was a clever scheme—while it lasted.

"Old man Luck was kinda with me and I found that .30-30 rifle, hanging in a tree; where it was easy to get, but hard to find. We had the pinto, the rifle, the telegram that put us in bad with the Fantom Riders.

"Folks, your cattle were never herded out of the Ghost Hills. They were loaded right into cattle-cars and shipped to market. They were loaded at night, shipped at night, and the crooked buyer falsified his reports, split the pot with a dirty coyote and his hired whelps.

"I know of three trains of Circle Cross cattle that were shipped out of Wolf Wells and the siding down the line; but Lanpher's reports show that only fifteen cars of stock were sold in one whole year. They—"

"Look out, Jim!" screamed Buck. "They've got us, damn their hearts!"

Buck's gun flashed in his hand and his first bullet smashed into the judge's desk beside Sleepy. The roar of his gun punctuated his screaming admission of guilt.

Trainor had flung himself sidewise, between Hashknife and the jury, which proceeded to lie down, fall down or to get out of line in any possible way, while Carsten drew a gun, seemingly out of thin air, and flung himself forward only to be met by Sleepy's first shot, fired from his hip.

Carsten pitched forward, his gun spinning out of his hand, while over his falling body whistled the lead from Hashknife's six-gun.

Trainor, with bullets thudding into his big body, laughed chokingly through the smoke and tried to make his nerveless finger pull the trigger of his big Colt. Then he went down sprawling on his face, his right hand still convulsively gripping the big gun.

Buck Avery had whirled and run to the rear after his first shot. He was seemingly bewildered as to what to do, but when he saw both

146 | W.C. TUTTLE

Carsten and Trainor down he sprang through the door out into the street, with Hashknife, Sleepy and the sheriff racing after him.

They reached the street, only to see Buck vault into a saddle and whirl his horse around. Hashknife fired a shot at him, but it was a clean miss. Buck was swinging his six-shooter up and down, as if trying to shoot back at them, when a horse and rider came out from between two of the buildings near Buck.

It was Poco Saunders, swaying weakly in his saddle, his reins dragging in the dust. A six-shooter dangled in his right hand and he seemed about to fall from his saddle; but at the sight of Buck Avery he straightened up and drove home his spurs.

Straight at Buck he went, and Buck waited for him, both shooting as they came together with a crash. Buck's horse went down from the impact, and Poco fell from his saddle; the riderless horse falling halfway to its knees and stopping dead still.

Hashknife was the first to reach them. Buck was dead; filled with bullets from Poco's gun. They turned Poco over and bolstered him against Buck's body; while the crowd poured out of the courtroom and surrounded them.

Poco was not dead, but he was going fast. He tried to grin up at Hashknife, and his voice was weak, as he said:

"Shot at you by accident, Hartley—this mornin'. Get Trainor, if yuh can. He's the head of the gang. Carsten is another. I helped 'em steal cattle, but I didn't have anythin' to do with the killin'. They didn't trust me and Smoky, I guess.

"Either Buck or Trainor killed Smoky, my bunkie. Buck tried to kill you. That drinkin' was all a blind, I think. I followed you and Stevens to the pinto and I seen you find the rifle, I laid for Buck. The rifle wouldn't shoot."

"Poco, I'm sorry," said Hashknife. "I like you, cowboy."

"Thank you, Hartley." Poco looked around at the crowd and tried to smile. "I reckon I'm all through. They can turn Ben Lanpher and Pinto Cassidy loose now. I—I'm just a damn rustler, Hartley; but I never killed from ambush. I can go clean. And I want yuh to know that Smoky wasn't in on the killin'. It was just Trainor and Buck."

"Trainor, Buck and Carsten won't do it again," said Hashknife.

Poco nodded shortly and lifted his head, as if listening, but his eyes were glazing fast.

"Somebody singin'?" he asked wearily. "What are they singin' about, I wonder? Why, I know that song. Gee, that's—"

Poco smiled, but this time the smile did not fade. Hashknife straightened up, his lips shut tightly, a sadness in his eyes, as he turned to the crowd.

"They're all Fantom Riders now, folks," he said and turned away toward the Lanpher family near the courtroom door.

Sleepy was talking to Lanpher, as Hashknife came up, and in a moment Ben Lanpher joined them. He had been turned loose.

"Here's m' prize pup-prisoner!" yelled Lonesome, and they turned to see old Pinto Cassidy coming from the jail, walking alone. He was also free. Lonesome was behind him, grinning from ear to ear, and doing a burlesque war-dance.

"That's damn good!" blurted Mrs. Cassidy hoarsely. "My man go home now."

"Sure, I dunno what it's all about," protested Cassidy, as Lorna threw both arms around his neck and her tears mingled with the stubble of his wrinkled face.

"My God, I'm thirsty," choked a lean-faced cowboy, who had been on the jury. He turned away toward a saloon, and several followed him.

"Hartley, I dunno what it's all about yet," admitted the sheriff. "Danged if it didn't happen so quick that I never even remembered that I had a gun. Why, Trainor never even fired a Shot. Gosh A'mighty, you two fellers sure do know how to make a gun hop."

The Lanphers surrounded them, trying to express their thanks but none of them could talk coherently. Ben shook hands with Hashknife silently and turned away to Lorna, who was with her father.

Lanpher was looking at them, as Hashknife touched him on the arm and spoke softly:

"Shoot square, Lanpher. This is between them."

"I know," breathed Lanpher. "It is not for us to say."

Mrs. Lanpher and Helen had moved in closer, watching Ben and Lorna, who were talking softly. Ben shook his head, as if not understanding. He questioned her anxiously, but she shook her head again and turned away.

Ben frowned thoughtfully.

"Will we be goin' home now, Lorna?" asked Cassidy huskily.

"Yes," she said softly, without lifting her head.

Ben looked at her for a moment and turned to his mother.

"She won't marry me," he said slowly.

"Why?" asked Mrs. Lanpher foolishly.

"She says she don't love me."

"Damn good reason!" blurted Mrs. Cassidy.

Cassidy crossed to her and put his arm around her; but she did not look up at him as she said:

"Love is such a little word, don't you see. It means today—not tomorrow or the next day. Ben wants to marry me today. His folks don't want him to marry me. He is willing to marry me in spite of them—today.

"I am half-Indian." She turned and faced them, her eyes half-closed. "Maybe the Indian half is the strongest. Ben would not love an Indian—tomorrow. And you will all be much happier. I want to be happy, too."

"Damn right!" exclaimed Mrs. Cassidy inelegantly.

"Well," Mrs. Lanpher gave a sigh of relief. "I'm glad it has all turned out for the best."

"Yes, for the best," said Lorna softly.

"But nobody has asked me what I think," complained Ben. "Haven't I anything to say about it?"

"Very little," said Cassidy. "Go on back to your town and settle down, Bennie. You've been a lucky lad to stay as long as ye have. Come, Lorna. Are ye ready, Minnie?"

"Damn right," said Minnie, "Momook klatawa."

Hashknife and Sleepy were watching Cassidy, Minnie and Lorna crossing the street, when Lanpher grasped Hashknife by the arm, yanking at him nervously.

"I'm still in a whirl," he declared. "It is like waking from a nightmare, don't you know it? Why, there isn't a man left on the Circle Cross. Four dead men! Can you imagine that?"

Hashknife nodded slowly, sadly. His face seemed to have aged years in a few minutes.

"Yeah, I can imagine it."

"Well, I don't know which way to turn."

Lanpher nervously fumbled in his pocket and produced a checkbook.

"I promised you a thousand apiece, didn't I? I'm going to double that. My Lord, it was worth three times that much. I—I mean, it is worth everything in the world to me."

Helen and her mother had come to them, and Lanpher turned nervously to them.

"I—I'm trying to pay my debts," he explained, showing them the check-book.

"In money?" asked Mrs. Lanpher.

"That's—right," Lanpher's voice softened and he shook his head. "Not my debts, mother—my bills."

He started to write a check, but stopped and looked straight at Hashknife.

"Hartley, will you and Stevens accept half-interest in the Circle Cross, and handle my half for me?"

"No, I reckon not," he said slowly, apologetically. "Yuh see, me and Sleepy have got so much iron in our system that we'd kinda rust if we hung around in one place too long. Thank yuh just the same, folks. It's a fine offer."

"Will you come to visit us at San Francisco?" asked Helen. "Our home is your home now."

"When you have a dry season," said Sleepy. "Fog and iron don't go well together."

"Where will you go from here?" asked Lanpher, handing them each a check. "We want to keep trade of you two."

"Keep track of us?" Hashknife smiled wistfully. "You'll have a job, pardner. We've been called the antidotes for poisoned ranges. We'll likely keep goin' until our medicine gets too weak. But we'll let yuh hear from us once in a while."

When Hashknife turned he found Sleepy grinning widely at him.

"What did Helen Lanpher mean, Hashknife?"

Hashknife grinned and rubbed his chin.

"I dunno," he confessed. "Did sound kinda funny. I wish it wasn't so danged drizzly in Frisco town."

"They have a dry season down there," said Sleepy suggestively.

"I s'pose. I'm havin' mine right now, cowboy. Let's bust these checks and hit the grit. I'm all fed up on tears, and I hate a quiet country like this. C'mon."

"It used to be a good country," sighed Sleepy.

Hashknife laughed softly, glanced back toward the hotel, and they rattled their spurs across the door step together.

www.ingramcontent.com/pod-product-compliance
Lightning Source LLC
Chambersburg PA
CBHW020650180626
46816CB00003B/1218